'I'm in the mood to again practise making a baby.'

June wanted to match her husband's bantering mood but found she could not. She turned her face away from the smouldering affection in his eyes. 'Stop it! It is not a game. Not to me,' she whispered in anguish. 'I know you are disappointed with me, however careful and kind you try to be over it all.'

After a tense silence William asked softly, 'Has it ever occurred to you, June, that perhaps I fret that *you* might be disappointed with *me*? It takes two people to make a baby.'

June noticed a painful solemnity in the profile presented to her. She had moved slightly away from him to properly see his expression, but now wanted to have him hug her again. When William made no attempt to bring her close she stayed still, feeling awkward and guilty. Tentatively she slipped a solitary finger over the broad hand, still beside her hip. She expected him to turn his fingers, to clutch at her conciliation. The only movement wa~~s in his face~~ ~~a muscle~~ tautened close t~~o~~

Dear Reader

The Meredith Sisters series was launched with *Wedding Night Revenge,* which charted the scandalous exploits of Rachel, the eldest of Edgar and Gloria Meredith's four beautiful daughters. In the ensuing novel, *The Unknown Wife,* Isabel took her turn to shock polite Society.

This third tale features gentle June and depicts the fortunes of her early marriage to William Pemberton. June is deemed to be the placid Meredith girl—and so she is, until her contentment is threatened...

The quartet of books will conclude with the youngest sister taking a starring role. Sylvie is a rebellious urchin, more than a match for a charismatic nobleman who arrogantly believes he can tame the silver-haired spitfire with his raw sensuality.

Four young ladies of differing character and interests, but the Meredith sisters are united in their courage and their resolve to win love and happiness. I hope you enjoy reading about how they succeed.

Mary Brendan

A SCANDALOUS MARRIAGE

Mary Brendan

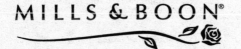

MILLS & BOON®

First published in Great Britain 2004
Paperback edition 2005
Harlequin Mills & Boon Limited,
Eton House, 18-24 Paradise Road, Richmond, Surrey TW9 1SR

© Mary Brendan 2004

ISBN 0 263 84355 6

Set in Times Roman 10½ on 13 pt.
04-0205-62794

Printed and bound in Spain
by Litografia Rosés S.A., Barcelona

Mary Brendan was born in North London and lived there for nineteen years before marrying and migrating north into Hertfordshire. She was grammar-school-educated, and has been at various times in her working life a personnel secretary for an international oil company, a property developer and a landlady. Presently working part-time in a local library, she dedicates hard-won leisure time to antique-browsing, curries, and keeping up with two lively sons.

Chapter One

'What an extraordinary coincidence!'

William Pemberton raised his distinguished head at his sweet wife's acid tone. Blue eyes that had been solemnly contemplating the brandy warming within his broad palm now met a glass-sharp gaze. It was a glancing contact, for her attention was already slicing past his shoulder.

'Your old friend is again socialising with us, William. Suddenly we appear to share many mutual acquaintances with Lady Bingham. She looks a little disappointed… Ah, but she has now spotted you and looks far less glum.'

'June…' William's weary sigh accompanied his wife's name.

June Pemberton bestowed on her husband a fleeting, bright smile. 'I shall not hamper your fond reminiscences this time, I promise. I was about to find my sisters, in any case.' June made to sweep away, her ivory skirts held in fingers so tightly clenched the delicate silk was imperilled.

'I have had enough of this interminable innuendo,' William gritted with a fierce azure look at his spouse from beneath heavy lashes. An unusually masterful hand on the soft skin of her arm stayed her. 'Accuse me or have done!'

'Accuse you? Of what, pray?' June countered, her complexion becomingly flushed. She was already regretting revealing that the elegant brunette, who had just entered the Cleggs' ballroom, had unsettled her to such a degree. Three times this week they had socialised. Three times Lady Constance Bingham had arrived shortly after they did, and on each occasion the pretty dowager had contrived at some point in the evening to corner William, in order to engage him in quite an intimate and cosy chat about the old days when once they had been *close*. And what worried June was she had recently discovered that once, indeed, they *had* been close.

In the previous few months Constance Bingham had limited her interest in William to lingering looks when their carriages passed on an afternoon drive, or a coquettish glance when they found themselves browsing the same parade of shops. In those early days, an arch comment from June congratulating her husband on his new allure had rendered him amused, then thoughtful, then murmuring that he believed she must be mistaken over it all. He had reminded her of his reputation as rather a dull fellow. She must look to her dashing brothers-in-law for gentlemen cast creditably in the role of gallant, he had told her with a wry grin that melted her heart. Thus, initially, she had felt an amount of pride that her William was drawing the attention of such a well-connected society lady.

But that was a month or more ago and Lady Bingham's interest was becoming insistent enough for others to notice and remark upon it. Not within June's hearing, of course; she was well aware that conversations sometimes dwindled on her arrival in an elegant drawing room.

Recently she had been on the point of demanding to know whether she was invisible, so blatantly had Lady Bingham been flirting with her husband, but angry tears had been too close to the surface for her to risk challenging the woman and making a fool of herself. Lady Bingham was making it clear she found her quarry's wife of no consequence, and that was galling. Dwelling on that truth now made her snap. 'Is it not coincidence then that Lady Bingham materialises at every social function we attend? And am I to believe it was simply good manners that obliged you to escort her to the terrace when she complained of feeling faint earlier this week?'

'God's teeth!' The oath was so explosive that a lady and gentleman close by slanted curious eyes at William's taut features. 'I believe I explained that incident at the time.' The words were enunciated through lips that scarce moved. 'Lady Bingham said she felt faint and asked me to accompany her outside for some air. Would you rather I had acted the boor and allowed her to collapse at my feet?'

June's amber eyes glowed tiger-bright as she dulcetly demurred. 'Indeed, no, sir. I would rather you had recommended she used her salts or, better still, went home. But whatever you *did* do to revive her certainly worked. When you later reappeared together she looked quite red in the face…radiant, I believe your mother put it when she drew my attention to you both.'

William closed his eyes and a low curse scratched at his throat. 'I might have guessed my mother would have some part in it. Come. We are leaving. I have had enough.'

'Too late, I fear.' His wife darted a look across his broad shoulder. 'Lady Bingham is being escorted to meet you by your parents.' With a flick of the wrist June had opened her reticule. A cold metal bottle was extracted and thrust into her husband's hand. 'Here! Take my hartshorn. Feel free to offer it to your admirer should she be in danger of swooning over you. 'Twould prevent a trip to the terrace and her risking pneumonia. That scrap she has on is positively indecent and will provide little protection against the night chill.' Without another word June turned and walked away.

William watched the ripple and sway of cream silk as his wife gracefully fled from him. The cascade of berry-blonde curls that curtained her nude sculpted shoulders glimmered in candlelight, stoking his frustrated desire. With a low sigh he forced his hungry eyes away. He hadn't investigated the approach of the people June had warned were nearby and, with rare incivility, avoided them by moving in the opposite direction. He felt unequal this evening to receiving any of his mother's studied bonhomie or Lady Bingham's coquetry. And he knew both were his if he remained where he was. But a quiet chat with his father would have been welcome. With a scowl moulding his mouth, he finished what was in his glass and weaved a path through a throng of people, hoping to find some uncomplicated male company.

As he walked he thought. He hadn't wanted to leave the house this evening, sensing this situation might arise, but June, with a *faux* gaiety, had evaded his amorous persuasiveness that they have a quiet night at home, and insisted they come. They had both known for some weeks that a confrontation about Lady Bingham's peculiar attention to him was imminent. A constant strain between them was upsetting their conjugal harmony, and thus William's equable nature.

William was coming to accept that his wife's suspicions were valid. Wherever they went, Constance was likely not only to materialise, but also to hound him. He knew too that June's mild annoyance at the woman's stalking had turned to a stronger emotion since they had become the butt of gossip. The fact that his own mother was fostering Constance's friendship and thus exacerbating the friction between him and June was obviously intriguing the *ton*. William, on the other hand, was well used to his mother's hostility to his wife.

'Is June ailing? She looked quite sickly, I thought, as she passed me a moment ago, with barely a greeting, too, I might add.'

William closed his eyes and blew a silent curse through his teeth on recognising the voice accosting him. It was wrong to have supposed his mother would give up pursuit quite so easily, even if Constance and his father had. On the edge of his vision he noticed his father leading Lady Bingham towards the supper room.

Pamela Pemberton fussily hoisted a flimsy shawl about her thin arms. 'Really, William! I think you ought have a word with your wife about her manners. Several years you have been wed; time enough by my reckoning for her early breeding to have been polished a little by association with us.'

William Pemberton gazed glacially at his mother. 'Yes, several years married, ma'am, and still she suits me as well as ever she did.'

Pamela sniffed. 'Still your nursery is empty. Where is my grandchild?'

'You have a granddaughter, as I recall… Hannah's child.'

'I have no daughter. I have had no daughter since she married that heathen.'

'Your choice, then, to have no grandchild either,' William pointed out, his voice vibrating with disgust. 'Your loss, too, for the little girl is beautiful and I'm proud to call her my niece.'

'That is understandable.' His mother theatrically sighed. 'Perhaps, if your wife suits you so very well, you must resign yourself to doting on other people's offspring.'

'Indeed I shall, if that is how it is to be.' William turned away from the sight of his mother's bitter, pinched features. 'We are going home. June is unwell and is just gone to take her leave of her sisters.'

'Going home?'

William removed the tenacious fingers that had fastened on his arm.

'But you have barely arrived. This is one of the

most lavish parties we shall see this season. You cannot go! Constance is here and keen to come to you.'

'Why is that?'

'Why is what?'

'Why is Constance keen to come to me? There are other people here she knows. Why single me out as a person on whom to bestow such favour?'

'Perhaps she finds you amusing…' The innocent simper that accompanied the remark was belied by the flush staining Pamela's cheeks. 'Oh, how should I know?' she blustered.

'I just thought you might, ma'am…' was William's parting shot as with a curt nod he moved on.

'If she's on the prowl for a husband now she's out of her widow's weeds, the least she can do is find one of her own.' Rachel Flinte, Countess of Devane, cast a belligerent glance at the back of Lady Bingham's coiffure as she made the remark.

'And it shouldn't be that difficult to attract one either, if rumours are true about what old Charlie Bingham bequeathed her,' Mrs Isabel Hauke contributed to the debate. 'Etienne said that it is rumoured he left her properties in three counties and a brace of ships docked in Bristol. Quite a lure for a gentleman with pockets to let.'

June looked at her two older sisters and gave a

wry smile. 'Thank you! I wish you hadn't told me that. She really is a catch. And besides…she is a very attractive woman, isn't she?'

Rachel shrugged dismissively. 'A person who favours Amazonian brunettes might think so.'

Isabel gave a toss of her mermaid hair. 'And William patently does not,' she roundly emphasised. 'The man's as besotted with you as ever he was. Since you left him moments ago his eyes have tracked you constantly. He looks…a little furious, June, not at all his usual suave self,' Isabel warned. 'And, now he's free of that witch of a parent of his, he appears to be heading this way.'

June unconsciously tidied her sleek blonde ringlets on learning that information. Her sister's description of the wealthy widow was rather uncharitable, she knew. Constance Bingham was attractively tall and willowy and her hair was a rich shade of chestnut. And June had recently learned that her husband *did* find Lady Bingham attractive…or once he had.

June's irritation over Lady Bingham constantly paying attention to William was transforming to jealousy since her mother-in-law had let her know that the couple had once been in love. But she found herself unable to challenge William over it, for had he not voluntarily mentioned his aborted betrothal to her himself several years ago?

William had been engaged to a Miss Palmer when he was twenty. He had told her that when first they met, and that Miss Palmer jilted him for a wealthier man. He had seemed philosophical about it all and reluctant to elaborate. It was just an inconsequential part of his youth, he had said on dismissing the affair. At that time June had not pressed him for further details of an alliance that had ended before they met, deeming it bad manners, and unnecessary. She had practically forgotten all about the matter, for why should it bother her? William had married her. William loved her. Just a few short months ago had he not told her so at least once a day, and again impressed it on her with sweet passion at night? But now a wedge of tension was nudging them apart.

Her mother-in-law had been good enough to satisfy her unspoken curiosity about the woman's past, and William's part in it. Constance Bingham, née Palmer, was returned to town from Devonshire and socialising again now her mourning for her late husband was done. Was June aware that William had almost married such a personable lady? Pamela Pemberton had asked with a satisfied twitch of a smile when her daughter-in-law's expression made it clear she was not. Since that time an icy feeling had been curdling June's stomach, for how blatantly the widow was parading in her face the fact that she still found her erstwhile fiancé attractive.

Isabel and Rachel exchanged a glance on noticing June's unhappy preoccupation. Her small teeth were sunk low in her bloodless bottom lip.

'If William wasn't such a perfect gentleman, I'm sure he would have by now made it clear that Constance Bingham vexes him.'

'Is he almost upon us?'

At her sister Isabel's discreet nod, June tilted her heart-shaped face. 'Well, smile, then. I won't have him thinking I'm a jealous shrew, even if I stupidly did act like one earlier this evening.'

'William!' Rachel greeted her brother-in-law and slipped a hand through his arm. 'Connor was looking for you earlier. I believe he went along to the card room thinking you might be playing at the tables.'

William gave his sisters-in-law a charming smile. 'Another time, maybe. June and I are leaving.'

June shot her husband a startled look. Her elfin face was animated by slashes of colour staining her cheekbones. 'How masterful you sound!' she playfully remarked. 'You will make Rachel and Isabel think I am to be taken home in disgrace. I would rather stay. We were about to find the supper room.'

As June made to link arms with her sisters and urge them on, William arrested her progress and drew her to his side. His head inclined intimately close to hers in the manner of a fond spouse. 'Most of these good people would love a little more reason to gossip over us, June,' was murmured into a delicate ear. 'Let us at least be in agreement over quitting this infernal place even if all else lately has us at odds. Here, make your malady look real and sniff your hartshorn, my love.'

June slid a look from beneath her luxurious lashes at her husband as he returned her the small silver bottle she had forced upon him earlier. Their eyes clung and his lips tilted in an engaging smile that mingled seduction and threat.

June felt her stomach tighten. She rather thought she knew how her husband would seek reconciliation once they were private tonight. Would she allow it? Her fair complexion tinged rose and her limbs were already a-tremble with anticipation. 'It seems I must be a dutiful wife then and oblige my lord and master.' Just a hint of sourness betrayed her lingering hurt.

William glanced at his sisters-in-law, who had diplomatically distanced themselves, before casting a trenchant look upon his wife. 'It would certainly be novel if you did, my sweet,' William drawled, with a significant irony that she understood and that made her blush deepen. 'It seems to me overlong since you obliged me in a solitary thing.' With his hand on her elbow and a nod for her sisters, he led her away.

A heavy frosty atmosphere that had little to do with the glittering pavements accompanied the couple homeward to Bay House in St James's. Once or twice June sought, with a fluttering glance, to decipher the expression on her husband's shadowy countenance. She had believed he might take her in his arms as soon as they were settled on the upholstery for the hand upon her waist, as he helped her into their carriage, had been wonderfully caressing. But, once seated, he had put his head back into the squabs and assessed the carriage roof as though stars were visible through it. Far from rebuffing his amorous advances, as she believed she would—until she had some reassuring answers from him over that shameless widow stalking him—she now found herself summoning the courage to slip on to his seat and cuddle up to him. June tilted up her chin. *She* was not at fault in this. Neither, she suspected, was William. But she felt fragile and vulnerable and in need of a little reassurance from the man she loved that she was cherished now, tonight, as surely as she had been a few months ago when Lady Constance Bingham, née Palmer, was blissfully unknown to her.

'It is a very cold night,' June remarked into the

silence with a peek out at the quiet whiteness. When a grunt was all the encouragement she received for her attempt at rapprochement, she snuggled into the seat and wrapped her arms about her.

Her husband's face was still angled upwards, his eyes half-closed, when she heard, 'Are you chilled?'

'Yes,' she eagerly answered.

William uncrossed his arms, opened them invitingly and with no further encouragement his wife hurtled gracefully into them.

William folded his great coat about June's slender body. Instinctively she curved against his side and was anchored there in a familiar way. Warm lips grazed across her cool forehead, while deft hands within the enveloping cloak warmed her silken limbs.

'What is happening to us, William?'

The sobbing little query made her husband groan and lift his petite wife atop his lap. A hand smoothed her cheek; his lips followed as he felt the wetness there. 'What is happening to us, June, is that we are allowing mischief-makers to meddle in our life. We must not allow them to succeed,' he whispered huskily. 'If that means choosing very carefully with whom we socialise, and where we go, then so be it.'

June nodded against his coat. 'You were right

earlier; we should have stayed home. I have not enjoyed one second of the Cleggs' ball.'

'We need not become recluses, but you know how gossips thrive if one seems affected by their malice. What else have the bitter souls to do but try to spread their misery?'

'Why does she hate me so? I have tried hard to please her and be a good daughter-in-law…' June choked.

William cupped tender fingers over his wife's jaw. 'And *I* have told you not to try so hard. You do not have to justify your status as my wife. She is my mother, that I cannot change, but you, I chose. You, I want. You, I will always want, no matter you came to me with little dowry and no aristocratic relations. Your father and mother are fine people. All your sisters I'm proud to call my sisters. My brothers-in-law I'm happy to do business with and call close friends. You suit me perfectly. You always have.'

'And your mother resents it, I know she does. She would have had you marry a nobleman's daughter…'

'Then she is a fool for not recognising *that* is exactly what I have done. I have married a very noble man's daughter.'

Chapter Two

'I had not believed William capable of such unmannerly behaviour till I witnessed it with my own eyes this evening.'

Alexander Pemberton shot his wife an ironic look. He dismissed the hovering servant with a weary hand-flick and discarded his overcoat on to a chair. Next he helped himself to the decanter. 'I perceived nothing unreasonable in our son's behaviour. I expect William considered a lack of gallantry appropriate tonight.' Alexander helped himself to a generous measure of cognac.

Pamela Pemberton, shrugging out of her pelisse, swivelled towards her husband, her arms imprisoned and mouth momentarily motionless. 'I'm sure I don't know what you mean by that.'

'I think you do, Pamela,' Alexander said quietly before he sipped. 'And I shall tell you something else: I shall not be a party to your schemes. Please do not again manipulate me into dancing attendance upon Lady Bingham as though I, too, approve of her peculiar interest in my son…my son, who is happily married to a woman he adores.' With unaffected chivalry Alexander helped his wife to extricate her arms from her coat and laid it aside for her.

Pamela snatched her satin sleeves about her in a way that her husband recognised, for it invariably presaged a tirade.

Alexander held up a silencing hand. 'And before you say one word, I have several more of my own I would have you listen to. Do not treat William as you do me: as though he were still a green youth likely to be swayed by your nagging. It is very many years since I observed him doing as you say, simply for a little peace and quiet. If you continue to meddle in his life, you will drive him completely away. I would bet a florin to get a crown that he is planning with June to repair to the country for the rest of the season, just so they might avoid any further unpleasant atmosphere.' Alexander cast a glance on his wife's indignant countenance and, as always, part of him softened for part of him still loved her. Gently he said, 'Do not underestimate William; he will not take kindly to being made to look a fool, Pamela.'

'How dare you lecture me over my son! Do you think I know nothing of his character? Naturally I want what is best for him. I have always wanted what is best for him.'

'If that is so, why are you helping to put him at risk of ridicule?'

'Ridicule? What are you talking about? *Ridicule*?' She illustrated her impatience and disbelief with a whirling hand.

Alexander slammed down his glass with unaccustomed temper. 'Tonight I heard Harley and Darlington smirking over a wager they've made that concerned our son and Constance Bingham. Lord Harley has it that William will have her as a mistress before Whitsun. Lord Darlington favours Constance holding out for a better offer from him and thinks Michaelmas might be when there is talk of a divorce. I am not saying their slander was sincerely meant; rather they seek to be jesters. I would have had both of them outside and told them exactly what I thought of their pathetic jokes had there not been over a hundred people present to witness the ensuing chaos. I'm quite sure that our son and daughter-in-law are aware they are being made the butt of hurtful gossip. Harley and Darlington haunt all the clubs and parties.'

Pamela had the grace to blush and stammer. 'I…I don't see how that is my fault. People have long memories. Obviously, some have remembered that William and Constance once were engaged…once they were in love.'

'If that is so, they must then also recall how enduring was her love for him. My own recollection is that, within a few months of my future daughter-in-law slipping on her engagement ring, she was replacing it with that flashy bauble Charlie Bingham gave her. Within an unconscionably short time she was Bingham's wife. Let us not mince our words over this, Pamela: Constance Bingham was a gold digger. William was hardly a pauper himself at that time, yet she wanted more. He couldn't give her a title, so with disrespectful haste she married a man who could.'

'She was browbeaten by her family,' Pamela quickly championed the widow. 'I can understand their ambition. I own I was angry with her when the betrothal was broke. But she *is* a baronet's daughter. It was natural her family would have favoured a more advantageous match for her. Lord Bingham was very wealthy and influential…and a nice gentleman, of course. Naturally, at his age, he wanted a speedy marriage and a chance to sire a male heir. Unfortunately it was not to be, but he has left her a very attractive prospect, and a daughter to love.'

'There is no nicer gentleman than our son,' Alexander said exceedingly quietly. 'Constance Bingham has had ample proof of it. If William were not such a courteous and tolerant character he would not give her the time of day, no matter what attractiveness or prospects she has. Do not help manoeuvre him into a situation, Pamela, where he is forced to relinquish his good manners to prove his love to his wife.'

'If June Meredith were a lady of proper refinement she would not make him act with incivility simply to flatter and placate her. She is behaving like a jealous minx, storming off like that when she knew we all were approaching to speak with him…and her. Why can she not conduct herself properly?'

'She is acting in the manner of a wife who is being exposed to humiliation and scandal through no fault of her own. And William is acting, not before time, like a man who is done with seeing upset the wife he adores.'

Pamela's mouth pinched. She stalked to the table and splashed cognac into a glass. 'Wife he adores?' she mimicked tartly. 'Why should *my* son be saddled with such a barren mouse? Had he and Constance wed he would have had children. She has already borne a fine daughter. I would bet a florin to get a crown she has many sturdy sons in her, too.

It is not to be borne that William might have no heir.'

'If he can bear it, my dear, I do not see why you cannot,' Alexander suggested drily. 'William and June have been married not yet four years; not so long when you think on it. Perchance they might prefer these early honeymoon years just for the two of them. They have plenty of time to start their family. In a decade they might have a sizeable brood.'

Pamela squinted at her spouse over the rim of a glass. 'What romantic drivel!' She gulped at her drink and coughed. 'Of course it is important to start one's family soon. She might first produce a quartet of daughters, as did her mother. She might need a half-dozen attempts before successfully producing a son. When one is well connected, one understands the great importance of continuing a noble bloodline,' she impressed on him, waving her empty glass.

'Ah, I might have known mention would eventually be made of the ducal connection. Your great-uncle on the distaff side might be a landed duke, but he is better known as a common sot. He has beggared himself in brothels and gaming houses, as well you know. The fact he has no male heir to inherit his debts and debauchery can only benefit society.'

Pamela, with tipsy gravity, smoothed her wispy hair, then licked the residue of alcohol from her desiccated lips. 'I have no intention of letting you rile me. You have long been envious of my superior lineage, I know.'

'You mistake the matter, my dear,' Alexander corrected quietly. 'What I have long coveted is my son's wisdom, for Lord knows how he did it with such wilful obstruction, but he managed to find himself the perfect wife.' Alexander caught up his coat in a smooth snatch and closed the drawing-room door quietly as he retired to his chamber.

Pamela stared after him for a long moment, her mouth compressed to a thin line. She went to the decanter and refilled her glass, then sought the warmth of the fire. The red in her cheeks had little to do with its glow.

Edgar Meredith took his wife into his arms. 'Come…come now, hush. I might have been mistaken. I wish I had not mentioned it to you at all.'

Gloria Meredith accepted the linen handkerchief proffered by her husband and dried her hot eyes, her leaky nose. 'I'm glad you did, Edgar.' She sorrowfully shook her head. 'I cannot believe it. It seems that the whole *ton* knows more about the state of one of my daughter's marriages than do I. I thought Constance Bingham just a silly fool. I thought her fawning over William nothing to worry about.'

'It *is* nothing to worry about, my dear—'

'How can you say that! There is gossip everywhere about a divorce, you say. And June and William looked to be at loggerheads this evening. At one point I'm sure they were arguing. Then they barely made time to come over and take their leave before they had gone. If they stayed an hour at the Cleggs' I should be surprised.' Gloria pressed the damp linen to her freshly streaming eyes.

'I did not say the *whole world* knows of it,' Edgar cooed. 'I overheard a conversation between two gentlemen in Boodle's and they were denouncing Harley's malicious lies as absurd. Most sensible people will dismiss them thus.' Edgar paused, a thoughtful look putting a crease between his eyes. 'But William is bound to be rightly furious when he finds out he and June are being pilloried. I hope he does not call Harley out...and he might with such provocation. He is a quiet gentleman; but then a mild manner sometimes conceals quite a dangerous adversary. I know he can fence and, if he shoots a pistol as well as he does a shotgun—he bagged more pheasant than any of us at Michaelmas—Harley will regret ever opening his mouth.' Edgar's enthusiasm for his son-in-law's sporting prowess tailed off as he heard his wife's unhappy little gurgle. 'There, there…dry your tears. Harley and his buck-toothed crony are just risible idiots, everybody says so.'

Edgar continued patting comfortingly at his wife's fingers until the tears glistening in her eyes were blinked away. 'Harley has never forgiven us since Connor made out of him a laughing stock over that game of cards, when I staked Windrush at the tables.' At his wife's piercing look of accusation, Edgar hurried on. 'Of course I would never have let him have it. I would have sobered up well enough to cheat if necessary to keep our home. But I knew Connor wouldn't let me down. He won the estate fair and square.'

'It is as well *that* son-in-law is also a fine gentleman, for I doubt many people would return such an asset to a man silly enough to lose it in the first place.'

'Yes…well…all in the past, all in the past…' Edgar quickly changed the subject, for the one he had stupidly settled on was a contretemps best forgotten. He relinquished past disasters and returned to the current family crisis. 'Harley would love to concoct a scandal about one of our daughters that was plausible enough to do us all harm.'

Gloria scrubbed her wet eyes. Oddly, the mention of other problems that had beset the Merediths rallied her courage. They had seen off trouble before and grown stronger for it. She sat straighter, and tapped lightly at the hand that rested on her arm, indicating Edgar's soothing was no longer required.

Creakily her husband straightened from his position, squatting by her chair.

'I suspect Harley and Darlington are not alone in weaving this tapestry of lies. Perhaps a female hand is dabbling in it too,' Gloria said with a meaningful squint at Edgar. 'Tomorrow I will call on Pamela Pemberton and she will see me if I have to loiter in her hallway all day. She has never accepted June, yet June has been unwavering in her loyalty. Just the other day June gave Rachel a scold for calling her mother-in-law a mean-spirited witch—an accurate description if ever I heard one. Naturally, I told Rachel off too, for it doesn't do to be *blatantly* disrespectful.' Gloria frowned in puzzlement. 'But then I wouldn't suppose she wished to expose her own son to scandal.'

Edgar expressed his bewilderment with a long face.

'Tomorrow I *am* going to see her.' Gloria blew her nose with some force and a pugnacious glint fired her bloodshot eyes.

'I think that unwise, Gloria,' her husband advised sagely. He took a turn about the sitting room, thoughtfully quiet. 'If William has heard the latest rumours, I dare say he is fuming. But to put your mind at rest I shall make it my business to see *him*. A little man-to-man chat is in order, I think.'

His wife appeared unconvinced of the success of that.

'Tongues would really start wagging if you ladies engaged in a cat fight over it all,' Edgar warned with a grin. 'And should Rachel insist in going along with you, that might just come to pass. You know what a vixen she can be when protecting her family.'

'I don't think she would do that, Edgar,' Gloria announced softly. 'Not now she is again increasing. I have not yet had an opportunity to tell you my glad tidings, so engrossed have we been in your bad news. I learned from Rachel just this evening that we are to be grandparents again. Catherine is to have a brother or sister and Marcus and Lydia are to have another cousin.' The mention of all their beautiful grandchildren at last put a smile on Gloria's lips. 'Isn't that wonderful news?'

Edgar beamed. 'Capital!' he breathed. 'Little wonder Connor is looking so uncommonly pleased with himself of late. When is the babe due?'

'Rachel thinks about September.' Gloria's expression became wistful. 'I know June will be so very pleased for Rachel and Connor, yet I fear to mention it to her. I know she says little on the subject, but I'm sure she would dearly love to announce similar news.'

'And so she shall, so she *shall*, my dear,' Edgar quietly, confidently assured his wife. 'All in good time June will have her family, you'll see.' He sighed. 'Of course, the mischief Harley is brewing is hardly likely to help at all with filling their nursery. It would need to be a most harmonious couple who could remain unaffected by learning there is a wager on the time of their divorce.'

Edgar put a finger to his lips, deep in thought. 'As I see it, the problem—if it is one—is that June and William are two people too nice for their own good. June has always been determined to be kind to all and sundry, even the undeserving, and her husband is the sort of fellow who would oblige you with his last sovereign. Such sweet-natured folk are bound to frustrate those malcontents who thrive on ill will.'

Gloria nodded agreement. 'Well, you may speak to the men first, but if nothing is done I will pay a visit on Pamela Pemberton. I will not have my June humiliated. I like William very much but he ought show his mettle over this.'

'He is looking grim; I feel sure his patience is at an end over it all,' Edgar championed his son-in-law.

'I noticed this evening he looked irritable,' Gloria said. 'I hope they have not gone home early simply to quarrel…'

With a tender sigh June buried her head against her husband's neck. A small hand slid over the hard ridges of muscle on his naked chest. Sated with pleasure, she slipped one of her silken legs between the brawny strength of William's, then sensually caressed it up and down. The fond tribute to his artful lovemaking made her husband angle his head and place a gentle kiss on her small nose.

'I'm sorry I was disagreeable earlier,' June whispered against warm skin.

'I would have you disagreeable every day if this is how you apologise for it,' William answered huskily. With gentle urgency he lifted her atop him and a hard hungry kiss reinforced the words. 'Why have we not done this for so long? Why have you made excuses for so long? I have been mad with desire for you.'

'I think you know the answer to that,' June muttered with a touch of acerbity.

'Constance Bingham is no threat to you, my love. She is probably desirous of a little flattery to boost her confidence now her mourning is at an end and she is again socialising. Soon she will be turning her attention to a more appreciative and unattached recipient. But…you would not have me act rudely towards her?'

'No! Of course not,' June said. 'It is just…I'm not sure she *will* turn her attention elsewhere. Besides, I rather think your mother might be disappointed if she did. I get the impression Pamela likes Lady Bingham. She regrets not having her as her daughter-in-law.' June pushed back from William, her fine hair draping his chest in a blanket of silk. 'I did not know that Constance Bingham is the Miss Palmer to whom you once were engaged. I would rather not have learned that from your mother. Why did *you* not tell me?' she demanded raggedly.

William smoothed a finger over a pale cheek. 'Why would I mention anything so insignificant? You are talking of a betrothal that ended over a decade ago. Our relationship endured for less than four months…or perhaps it was five. I cannot now recall.' A careless grimace transformed effortlessly into a fond smile. 'In the fullness of time I found you and I married you. I have no regrets at all. I love you.'

'Once you loved Constance.' When silence was all the response she got, June probed. 'You did, didn't you? Or was it a convenient match?'

'I'm not sure there was love between us, but it would have been financially convenient…' He sighed and put a hand across his eyes. 'I don't see that there is any point in pondering the matter now, June. I was barely twenty…still a green boy. The matter is finished.'

'Perhaps Constance would like to revive it. Perhaps your mother would like that, too. Lady Bingham has a daughter. One of the reasons you mother is disappointed with me is because you are not yet a father.'

William sat up, lifting his wife with him so she was settled on his lap, enclosed in a warm embrace, while he rocked her soothingly. The memory of his mother's bitter words over June's failure to conceive had simply fired his disgust for her and his protectiveness for June. 'If—when, God willing, we have children, then it will be wonderful…for us.' He gave his wife a seductive smile. 'Perhaps it is just that we need a little more practice to get it right. I might let you persuade me to try again now…' He smothered his wife's laughing response with his mouth as he lowered them both back to the bed.

Hours later in the dark, June whispered, 'Are you awake?'

Her husband grunted a sleepy response.

'I have been thinking…we should not let malicious people intimidate us. We shall not scuttle away to Grove House,' she said, mentioning their country estate in Essex. 'We shall stay here, and enjoy the season and socialise with whomsoever we please. We have nothing to be ashamed of.'

William murmured assent and cuddled his wife against his shoulder before whispering, 'Very well… Now, unless you are prepared to practise again…go to sleep.'

Chapter Three

'That is wonderful news. Oh, Rachel, I'm so pleased for you and Connor.'

'You would have known last night when I told the others…but you and William left so early…'

'It is obviously but a tiddler at the moment.' June gave Rachel's flat abdomen a fond pat. But she felt quite a fraud for appearing so jolly and sincere, for behind her congratulations and her smile was an ache of envy.

Rachel and Connor had been married just a few weeks before she and William, yet already her sister and brother-in-law were fortunate enough to be awaiting the birth of their second child. A disagreeable self-pity was consuming her, and such base emotion made her ashamed. It was not her sister's fault that she and William had yet to experience the excitement of impending parenthood.

Quickly June turned away to compose herself. She found the teapot and poured herself a cup, obliquely aware that her mother and her sister Isabel were discreetly gauging her reaction to Rachel's news. Their anxious sympathy increased her turmoil; her eyes filled with tears. Banishing the heavy silence with some light conversation might have helped her humour, but the lump in her throat made speech impossible.

June gulped at her tea, relieved of the necessity of searching her mind for some mundane conversation. Gratefully she settled on observing some people newly arrived in the room. Close behind her strikingly blonde sister Sylvie came two distinguished dark-haired men. Connor Flinte, Earl of Devane, and Colonel Etienne Hauke were her elder sisters' handsome husbands.

But it was Sylvie, at sixteen, the youngest of Edgar and Gloria Meredith's four daughters, who captured all eyes, as she made her chaotic entrance into the sitting room. Sylvie's sculpted little chin was tossed back, tumbling tresses glinting silver in sunlight as she angled her head away from an attack by the creature she had imprisoned.

Gloria's jaw dropped in horror. 'What on earth are you doing with that?' she cried, glaring at two glass-bright beady eyes and a pecking beak.

'It has an injured wing,' Sylvie explained, with

a finger soothing a bony dome of a head. 'One of Isabel's cures might help the poor thing. It beat off Tabitha.' It was announced in admiration, for the cook's cat was a hunter par excellence.

'Take it to the garden at once!' Gloria exploded. Her furiously flapping hand created a draught and the ruffled bird deposited ample evidence on her rug that it indeed ought to be outside.

Connor arched an amused eyebrow at his brother-in-law. 'Will you or shall I?'

'You…I insist…' Etienne answered, all rueful courtesy, and grinned as Connor gingerly extricated the jumpy pigeon from Sylvie's clutch and headed for the terrace with it.

'Oh, Connor! Don't put it back in the open!' the Earl's young sister-in-law wailed. 'Tabitha will eas-·ily search it out. And it is cold…it might perish.'

'I'll find Bruce,' Connor promised soothingly, nominating one of the young grooms who kept all manner of wildlife as pets. 'I am sure he can find somewhere snug and warm for it.'

'Probably his oven,' Etienne muttered to his wife with a wicked smile. Isabel gave him a warning frown, but couldn't prevent a low chuckle at the thought of the plucky fugitive ending in a pie.

'You must get ready to go out, young lady,' Gloria instructed. 'You need material for gowns. You need hats, shoes, all manner of accessories.'

'I don't want a début ball, Mama.' Sylvie sighed. 'I have said so enough times.'

'You *will* have your come-out, young lady, for I would rather you scandalise society with your antics after having at least been launched into it.' At her daughter's mutinous look, Gloria snapped, 'You're fortunate Rachel and Connor have offered to give up their afternoon to escort you.'

After a moment Rachel followed her sulky sister into the hall, muttering that she had best hurry her along for, left to her own devices, Sylvie would not be ready to quit the house before the warehouses were closing for business.

Gloria sank back into her chair as silence reigned. 'That girl jangles my poor nerves like nothing else. Why is she not as other young ladies approaching seventeen? Why is she not giggling with friends over handsome young men? She is happier visiting the circulating library than the newest fabric emporiums.'

June went to her mother's chair and held still her fluttery hand to fondly chafe it. 'She is the baby of the family, Mama, and we have all woefully indulged her. She is just a mite immature and does love her pets. Be thankful she has got over her phase of wanting to tramp the jungle in Africa as a missionary. Instead of a wood pigeon in the house, it might have been a snake or spider.'

'You are right,' her mother agreed, appalled. After a brief fidget, Gloria was again up on her feet. 'Oh, I shall not rest if I don't go, too. Sylvie is bound to cajole her sister into letting her have a fright of a hat or material for a gown that wouldn't disgrace a Haymarket strumpet. And I'd best find a servant to clear up that mess…' With wrinkled nose and a finger waggling in disgust she drew eyes to the stain on her carpet.

June watched her mother bustling from the room. The past few chaotic minutes had, oddly, lifted her depression. Inwardly she gave herself a little scold for having given way to resentfulness over Rachel's happy news. She then offered up silent thanks for her youngest sister's tomboy ways. Sylvie could always be relied upon to create a drama wherever she went, and to do so with an air of heedless innocence that somehow charmed all that came close.

June turned to the sister who remained in the room with her, and noticed a significant look passing between Isabel and her husband.

'I think I shall find Edgar and his decanter and beg a restorative. I need it after all the excitement,' Etienne duly announced with a grin.

Guessing that Isabel wanted to resume their last conversation about Constance Bingham, June sought for an alternative. She and William had left the Cleggs' ball looking quite clearly at odds with one another. It was no wonder that her family would be anxious for her happiness. But now that they had tackled the subject of the preying widow, and William had sweetly allayed her fears on that score, she didn't want to think about the wretched woman, let alone discuss her. 'Poor Mama,' June blurted, as Etienne shut the door and she and Isabel were left private in the serene, sunny morning room. 'She will insist on Sylvie having her come-out this season. I think waiting another year or so might benefit her…character…and her prospects, don't you?'

Isabel grimaced with wry amusement. 'I think our poor parents would rather find an obliging gentleman to take Sylvie off their hands as soon as may be. She might do something utterly outrageous and really ruin her chances. She shouldn't have too much of a problem attracting a dozen or more admirers with that face.'

'It is as well she is a beauty,' June remarked. 'She is seventeen this year, after all, and we must all correct her more and tolerate her less. It is bad of her to aggravate Mama so.' June paused and chuckled. 'How righteous I sound!' she mocked herself. 'I think Mama would say we have all been an equal worry, in our own ways.'

'Not you,' Isabel said softly. 'You, my dear, are widely known as the *sensible* Meredith girl. I'm sure our parents have always been content with your goodness and sweet nature. And you married William without any hint of scandal attached to the match, which naturally they very much appreciated.' Isabel lifted an eyebrow, a wry hint at the shocking events that had besmirched her spinsterhood. Neither had Rachel managed to attain the married state minus notoriety.

'But that is the point, Isabel, I am *not* all goodness. My nature is *not* sweet at all,' June insisted. 'Sometimes, I hate myself, and my selfish thoughts.' Following a moment's indecision, June confided, 'I envy you and Rachel so much that it makes me quite unkind. I know I shouldn't be like that… But I would dearly love to be able to announce to our parents that *I* am to give them a grandchild. I felt horribly bitter when Rachel told me her wonderful news. You see, I can be very mean.'

With a murmured, 'No, not at all!' Isabel was up and out of her chair. June's shrinking figure was drawn comfortingly into an embrace. 'It is natural you would be upset. You must not feel ashamed that you yearn to be a mother!'

'I do feel ashamed,' June gruffly admitted, shielding her wet eyes. 'I long to tell William he is to be a father. I know it is news every husband expects to hear from his wife. I feel I have failed him—'

'You have not! He has not said so, has he? You didn't quarrel with William when you got home yesterday, did you?'

A secret little smile slowly smoothed June's melancholic countenance. 'No, he never blames me. And, no, we did not really quarrel at all…quite the reverse…'

'Well, that is a step in the right direction to getting your baby.' The insinuation and saucy smile that accompanied Isabel's remark put a bloom in June's ivory cheeks.

Her sister's sincere concern and sympathy prompted June to open her heart. 'William's mother despises me because I am not yet increasing. William's sister, Hannah, has given her a granddaughter but she won't have anything to do with them because her husband is related to Romanies. Why is she so unkind? Toby is very good to Hannah and their little girl. She is three years old and adorably polite.'

'Pamela Pemberton will never be content,' Isabel interjected pithily. 'I do not know her as well as you, but I imagine being miserable is the breath of life to her. She will always find some fault to pick on. If you had a brace of healthy sons, for her, they would be too dark or too fair, too tall or too short.

It is in her nature to be contrary. You must not let her worry you, June. If you are tense and anxious, it will not at all help you get the baby you long for.'

'Sometimes I think I have got him,' June volunteered softly. 'Then my menses come late. Sometimes they do not come at all for a month or two. But always, eventually, they come.'

'Oh!' Isabel turned her eyes heavenwards in exasperation. 'It is a shame you did not share that news sooner. I could prepare you a herbal remedy for the irregularity,' she offered. 'It has been known to help in other ways too, as a tonic.'

'Yes…I thank you. I suppose there is no harm in trying it.' Isabel was a talented herbalist, yet June looked a little unconvinced. Nevertheless she smiled in gratitude.

Isabel gave June's arm an encouraging shake. 'I am sure it will help for it has an added benefit…as a love-potion. Take no more than I recommend or you will quite wear out poor William!'

Edgar took a turn about his study, pretending to read the documents in his hand. The paragraphs were a meaningless blur so he yielded to temptation and peered myopically over wire rims at his son-in-law. He ferreted about for a few appropriate words with which to launch into the delicate subject of this fellow's domestic tribulations. June was a beloved daughter, but she had passed into the care of this man several years ago and Edgar had never previously felt anything but gladdened by that arrangement. Yet he had promised Gloria he would speak to William, so speak to him he must.

William was stationed close by the window in Edgar's study. After sipping at the fine Madeira his wife's father had pressed into his hand the moment he arrived, William turned his cerulean gaze to drift over the lime trees just coming into bud along Beaulieu Gardens. A brief smile moved his mouth for he was conscious of Edgar's observation and his predicament. He knew his father-in-law had summoned him here, not to comment on the performance of the stock portfolio bunched in one of his fists, but to interrogate him over rumours he had heard. Edgar was concerned for his daughter's happiness, which was as it should be. William had always liked and respected Edgar. Connor would always be Edgar's favourite son-in-law but he treated Etienne and William with affection. However, even had they hated one another, William realised he would have still asked the man for his daughter's hand in marriage. Almost four years wed and June still had the power to stir his blood with her sensual-shy smile.

William turned abruptly from the window, making Edgar glance away swiftly. He shook the papers in his hand in a businesslike manner and brought them closer to his bespectacled vision.

'I'm glad you invited us here today. June has not seen her sister Sylvie in some weeks. It also gives me an opportunity to have a private word with you. A ridiculous bit of gossip about June and me is in circulation,' William opened proceedings.

Relief was apparent in Edgar's face as he carefully extricated his spectacles from his ears. The pair of glasses and the sheaf of papers were dropped to his desk before he gave William his full attention.

'I imagine you have also heard the rumours and have refrained from commenting on them because such absurdity is beneath notice or contempt. Nevertheless, I want to put your mind at rest. I will do my utmost to protect June from the harm the instigator of such vile lies intends.' William's tone and expression were frank and sincere.

Edgar nodded sagely. 'I'll admit that I have heard some talk of a wager between Harley and Darlington…the two buffoons. Harley is too far into his cups of late. He was found in a gutter in Shoreditch just last week. He'd lost his cash and other valuables and, by all accounts, it was only his coachman's lucky arrival that saved the clothes disappearing from his back. It's a shame the miscreants spared his skin.' Edgar's tone was uncharacteristically vicious.

'He is not worth your anger,' William stated quietly.

'The blackguard needs horsewhipping,' Edgar spat, unappeased. 'He has antagonised too many people over too many years. It is not the first time our family have clashed with him. It makes my blood boil to let him get away with it.' Edgar sent a shrewd look flitting over William's pacific demeanour. 'Perhaps we ought to have a word with your brothers-in-law about it. Connor and Etienne have said nothing to me, but they must be aware of the gossip. They will not like it that June is being upset…'

'*I* do not like it that my wife is being upset,' William interjected. He had spoken exceedingly quietly, yet every word was clearly enunciated. 'Do you think I cannot protect my own wife from such as Harley?' The query was mild, a little short of amused.

Edgar had the grace to blush. 'No, of course I do not. I meant no offence. It is just that Connor and Etienne are military men. They are used to… umm…acting aggressively when necessary,' Edgar explained in a rush. 'You, William, have led a quiet and perfectly blameless life.' He endorsed his conciliatory compliment with a proud beam.

William's lips twitched in response. 'Thank you for the offer to find such assistance, but, quiet and blameless as my life might have been, I will fight this particular battle, should it come to that. At the moment I am loath to give credence to the gossip by challenging Harley over it. I think it best not to dignify absurd slander with any such attention.'

Edgar nodded agreement whilst subjecting William to a penetrating stare. 'Do you think these rumours of a divorce have been fuelled by the fact that…?' He hesitated, stuck his fingers between his neck cloth and his bobbing Adam's apple. 'Do you think it has come about because your nursery is still empty?' he rattled off.

William frowned, and looked genuinely puzzled. 'It is a possibility, although I admit it had not occurred to me. But then I admit, too, it had not occurred to me that vicious-minded people would try to cause us trouble. I think I can honestly say that June and I have never knowingly made enemies.'

'You and June are fine people…fair people.' Edgar emphasised his admiration with a quivering fist in the air. 'Your good natures rankle misanthropes. How pitiful must their lives seem when they witness how happy and popular you and June are.' He took a turn about the room, slowing to stub a foot against the fender. 'This is not easy to say, for I know once you were close to her… Do you believe that Lady Bingham might have a hand in stirring this particular pot? It is obvious she…umm…she still likes you.'

William shook his head. 'I think such scheming would be beneath her. Constance simply hankers after flattery. She must be sadly disappointed in having wasted time on me.'

'Don't be too modest, my boy. She seems to me a woman with regrets. Even without your mother's encouragement, I think Constance Bingham might still trail in your wake.'

William grimaced a sigh. 'I deduce that you think my mother is making mischief.'

'Perhaps your father will speak to her…just a cautionary word that it is being noticed how well she favours Constance.' Edgar refrained from saying that it was becoming common knowledge that Pamela Pemberton preferred the lovelorn widow to her own daughter-in-law.

'Perhaps he will,' William returned evenly, yet he was aware of what remained unspoken between them.

Edgar cleared his throat. 'Please don't think I am prying, but I would hate this gossip to propel you and June into constant arguments.'

William's head tipped back and he frowned at the ceiling. 'Naturally Constance's odd attention to me has not pleased June.'

Edgar frowned. 'Of how much is June aware? Has she heard that Harley is spreading rumours of a divorce?'

William looked sharply at his father-in-law. With uncharacteristic vehemence he blasphemed beneath his breath. 'I hope she has not. I'm convinced she cannot know or our household really would now be set on its ears.' He looked off into distance, his jaw set solid as stone. 'I shall tell her soon for I do not want her hearing of it elsewhere. It is very new tattle in the clubs, but it will soon spread to the drawing rooms.'

'Oh, yes,' Edgar concurred with heavy irony. 'Once those gentlemen's ladies get wind of it, it will spread like wildfire.'

William nodded. 'I'll tell her soon,' he repeated quietly.

'I just spotted Connor out of the window in your father's study. Why is he carrying about a fat pigeon?'

June gave Isabel a look and, simultaneously, they burst out laughing. Catching her breath, June said to her newly arrived husband, who was in the process of closing the sitting-room door, 'Come, let us take advantage of the sunshine this morning. You promised to take me to the opera this week and I haven't one decent shawl to match my blue gown. Let's go shopping in the landau and I shall tell you all about Sylvie's latest escapade.'

Chapter Four

'I recognise that fellow over there. I wish I could recall where I know him from.'

June peered through dim light in the direction that her husband had indicated and saw, in an adjacent box, a tall, dark-haired gentleman laughing with a rather showy and tactile female companion. June shrugged her ignorance of the man's identity and settled back. Within a moment, exhilaration had her once more on the edge of her seat, keenly observing a seething scrum of humanity in the theatre pit. She idly looked back at the person William thought he knew and noticed he was turned their way, his opera glasses raised, obscuring his eyes.

'I believe that gentleman has spotted you too, William,' she told her husband just as the strains of the orchestra filled the air.

A thousand conversations ebbed into silence as

a flow of pastel-clad dancers shimmered on to the stage. Entranced by the magic, the assault on the senses of sweet music, swaying bodies, June twined her slender hand into her husband's long fingers. The immediate welcoming pressure from William, the warmth of his familiar skin, had her snuggling back blissfully into her chair. Four years wed to this man and still with a look or a touch he had the power to twinge her insides with mingling excitement and longing. Her anxieties over Lady Bingham seemed just so much silly hysteria. Soon, she promised herself, every bad thing would simply melt away. So blissful did she feel that, just as the soprano swelled to sing, she whispered, 'Rachel is to have another baby. Isn't that wonderful news?'

William slanted her a lingering look that bathed her in adoration. A low-lidded smile and the increasing pressure of his hand on hers told her he was equally happy for the couple. At the second attempt he managed to drag his eyes back to the nubile dancers flaunting their charms.

'William Pemberton, if I'm not very much mistaken. And this, I take it, is your lady wife?'

William turned about as an affable cultured voice hailed him. An arm about June was keeping her close to his side, shielding her from the crowd clogging the corridors and stairs of the Theatre Royal during the opera's interval. After a frown, William's blond head tipped back and a bark of laughter was followed by, 'Adam Townsend! Hell and high water! It's been some years since I saw you! How many is it, do you think? Eleven? Twelve?'

'More than I care to count,' the man responded with a wry grin.

William turned to June. 'Here before you, my dear, is one of my old friends from school. We were at Eton together, then I went to Cambridge and this scoundrel defected to Oxford before going off to explore exotic lands.'

'Is he a scoundrel for choosing Oxford, or for exploring exotic lands?' June asked. 'Or perhaps he is simply a scoundrel,' she murmured archly. June smiled up at the tall gentleman, judging him rather nice and decidedly handsome, too!

'I must answer that, ma'am, for I don't want to be bad friends with your husband if he is too honest. As we haven't seen each other in more than a decade I'd like to have a chat with him over a good cognac rather than call him out. I must confess I've been a bit of a rogue, but only when in like company.' He clapped a hand on William's shoulder. 'Needless to say, I'm presently on my best behaviour. This fine fellow always exerted a civilising effect on us all. My mother used to like him very much. In fact, not that long ago, she asked whether

I had set eyes on him. Obviously she deemed me in need of his worthy influence.'

'How is Lady Rockingham?' The fondness in William's tone made June take a look at her husband.

'She is not in the best of health. But then she is still well enough to ride to hounds on occasion, so I accuse her of being a fraud.' Adam suddenly cast June an admiring look. 'If I'd known that you had married such a beautiful lady, Pemberton, I might have come looking for you sooner. You're a very lucky man. Has she any sisters?'

June blushed prettily at the compliment.

William drawled, 'When are you returning to those exotic lands, Townsend? Soon? I think you should.'

'Not just yet, I'm afraid,' his friend responded with an impenitent grin. 'By the by, have you seen Blackmore? I was astonished when I clapped eyes on him. Someone told me—can't remember who—that he had bolted for the Americas some years ago. But he is here, tonight, large as life and looking better than I remember he ever did.'

'Blackmore? Gavin Blackmore?' At his friend's nod, William turned to June with a rueful, 'I'm sorry, my dear. We venture out for a romantic evening at the opera and it turns into a school reunion.' To Adam he said, 'I haven't seen him either since we all went our separate ways. I'm not sure I would recognise him if I did.'

'Oh, you'd recognise him. He has a more affluent look, but his plebeian swagger is unchanged.' At the clatter of feet over the stairs that heralded the start of the second act he added quickly, 'I'd be obliged if you both would honour me with a visit soon. I'm staying at my house in Upper Brook Street for a while.'

At June's happy nod of assent, he gave a courteous bow. To William he said, 'Fancy a game of faro in Boodle's tomorrow? We could mull over old times.'

'I look forward to it,' William answered.

'Your friend appears to be trying to catch your eye,' June helpfully mentioned to Mr Townsend as she saw the flashy woman he had been conversing with earlier ducking this way and that to try and attract his attention.

Adam took a glance to his left. His eyes skimmed William's and a corner of his mouth tugged into a smile. He bowed again, all innocent politeness, and was gone.

June watched his imposing figure retreating until it was lost to view in the crowd. 'He seems an interesting gentleman. I have never heard you mention him, William, or that other friend—Gavin

Blackmore, was it? In fact, you have told me little of your schooldays.'

William shrugged. 'My schooldays are a long time ago. I can barely recall much about them. I'm nearly thirty-one, you know…almost middle-aged,' he lamented.

June gave him a sultry sideways look. As they walked back to their box her regard turned into strengthening subtle assessment. William had spoken modestly, as always. Yes, he had entered his thirties, and to her he looked ever more handsome. His eyes were still an intense blue and the fine lines the years had settled on his countenance gave him a charismatic worldliness. His fair hair shone with silver close to his ears and that too suited him. It was distinguishing rather than ageing. William's father, Alexander Pemberton, was one of the most handsome men amongst his sexagenarian peers. He had retained his tall stately bearing and his thick hair, once blond, was now a fine shade of steel. June imagined that William would look much the same as his father when in his sixties. An odd and forlorn feeling crept over her and analysing it made her catch her breath, for it was born of an uncertainty whether she would still be close to him to witness it.

At the touch of loving fingers caressing her neck beneath soft tumbling curls June's eyelids drooped.

Instinctively she snuggled closer to her husband as they journeyed home in their comfortable carriage. 'Do you think we should have tarried a little after the performance for you to look for your other friend?'

'No.'

'Why not? Was he not a close friend?'

'I'd rather we went straight home.'

At the subtle seduction in his voice June peeped from beneath a luxurious fringe of lashes and asked coyly, 'And why is that?'

'Because I'm in the mood to again practise making a baby.'

June wanted to match his bantering mood, but found she could not. She turned her face away from the smouldering affection in his eyes. 'Stop it! It is not a game. Not to me,' she whispered in anguish. 'I know you are disappointed with me, however careful and kind you try to be over it all.'

After a tense silence William asked softly, 'Has it ever occurred to you, June, that perhaps I fret that *you* might be disappointed with *me*?'

'Disappointed with *you*?' June echoed, an odd mocking note in her voice. 'Disappointed with my perfect William? What could you possibly lack?'

William ignored her petulance. 'It takes two people to make a baby. Perhaps the fault is not with you. Do you think that has not occurred to me?'

June noticed a painful solemnity in the profile presented to her. She had moved slightly away from him to properly see his expression, but now wanted to have him hug her again. When William made no attempt to bring her close she stayed still, feeling awkward and guilty, with her head bowed and tears needling her eyes. Tentatively she slipped a solitary finger over the broad hand, still beside her hip. She expected him to turn his fingers, to clutch at her conciliation. The only movement was in his face as a muscle tautened close to his mouth. As the tense silence protracted June shifted to her corner of the carriage and watched the dusk through blurry vision.

'If you're waiting for my sister June, she will be an age yet. She has trod on the hem of her gown and torn it. It will take her an hour at least to decide what next to wear.'

Adam Townsend dropped the hand that propped his chin and turned to see who had spoken. The grubby goddess just inside the door ventured further in, staring boldly at him with an unbecoming inquisitiveness. Shifting position from where he had been lounging against the marble mantel, Adam summoned up a smile while thoughtfully studying the angelic chit. Her sweetly curving body proclaimed her a young woman; her dishevelled pink attire and her attitude proclaimed her just a precocious child.

'Ah, you must be Sylvie,' he said pleasantly. 'William said his wife had a younger sister who was visiting today.'

'It's not my proper name,' she informed him. 'My real name is Silver. My mother named us all for what caught her fancy when we were first born. My eldest sister is called Rachel for Mama then read Bible stories. Isabel arrived at a time when she liked learning about the Spanish court. June Rose was born in the summer, naturally, and my mama's bed was close to the window…the ramblers are right up to the eaves at Windrush.'

Adam looked at a tumble of polished platinum tresses spilling almost to her tiny waist. 'And when you were born your beautiful hair caught your mother's eye…'

Her frown told him she was piqued at being deprived of concluding her tale of Meredith family eccentricity.

'Do you not like the name Silver? I think it rather nice.'

A shrug answered him. 'When I was little, I could only say my name as Sylvie. So I have always been Sylvie.' She walked further into the room and, head cocked to one side, looked him up and down. 'You came here a few days ago to take June for a ride. I saw you through the window. Is that your curricle? It's very flash.'

Adam nodded, confused, for he wasn't sure whether he would have the odd minx go or stay. There was something about her that fascinated him. Perhaps the fact that she was so easy on the eye explained it.

'Why isn't William taking June for a carriage ride? I hope they haven't quarrelled again.'

A small frown met that artless announcement. Adam answered diplomatically, 'William has urgent business with his attorney. I requested the pleasure of taking Mrs Pemberton for a ride in the park this afternoon.' He studied the exquisite features turned up to his. She met his stare unblinkingly. Suddenly he was blushing and the experience was so novel that he felt a further surge of blood to his head.

It was a unique experience to have such a perfectly beautiful young lady peer directly at him with no hint of coquetry. He was used to fans and eyelashes stirring in his presence, signalling a young lady's interest in his eligibility. Silver's candid curiosity made him fear that, not only did he not appeal, but that he might suddenly have sprouted horns. Feeling oddly unsettled, he shoved himself away from the mantelpiece and looked at the door. As if in answer to his prayer, it opened.

'Have you been keeping Mr Townsend company, Sylvie?' June asked as she stepped, perfectly attired in amber velvet, into the room.

'I explained you ripped your skirt. I thought you'd be ages yet. May I come for a ride in the curricle with you?'

'No, you may not, young lady. Mama is expecting you upstairs. Madame Bouillon is coming soon to give you a fitting.' June ignored Sylvie's laboured sigh. With a smile at Adam's expression— an odd mix of regret and relief—June indicated to her urbane escort that she was ready to go.

'Your young sister seems quite a...forthright young lady.'

'Oh, yes,' June concurred on a smile. 'She can also be rather...gauche at times.'

'I noticed,' Adam replied ruefully. 'How old is she?'

'Older than she seems,' June returned. 'I should warn you, when she sets her mind to it, she can be perfectly charming. Nevertheless, it is hard to believe that she has her seventeenth birthday in two months.'

The astonishment arching her companion's

brows beneath his dark hair was almost comical to behold.

'Our parents are hoping to launch her into society this season. Sylvie is reluctant to relinquish her life as a tomboy. Hence her lack of interest in having her new dresses made ready. As the baby of the family she has been spoiled—I suppose it is unfair of us all to expect her to undergo a miraculous transformation on her seventeenth birthday and emerge as a demure débutante.'

Adam chuckled. 'Indeed, that would be a miracle…and not necessarily an improvement.'

June slanted him a curious look, dismissed the notion as absurd and tucked a curl behind her ear. She ran a hand over the curricle's glossy green coachwork. 'It is such a mild afternoon for this time of the year.' After a few minutes of harmonious quiet she added, 'It was a piece of good luck that you and William met at the Opera after so long a gap in your acquaintance. But I'm glad you did. I have enjoyed our two excursions. I was hoping that we might also meet the other friend you mentioned that night…Jason Blackwell…' she suddenly burst out, pleased at having dredged the name from her memory.

'Oh, you mean Gavin Blackmore,' Adam amended lightly. 'If you really want to meet him, let us take another turn about the park for we passed him some ten minutes ago by Hyde Park Corner. I can't say I'd usually go out of my way to seek him out.'

June peered over her shoulder back towards the portals to the park. She recalled her escort had lifted a lazy hand to acknowledge an acquaintance as they drove towards the entrance. In her mind's eye was a gentleman who was fairly unremarkable, although he had looked at her with the sort of penetrating masculine interest that was complimentary, if a little stark. June gave Adam a quick look, for he had not sounded very enthusiastic about the fellow. She remembered he had made a rather barbed comment about him when they first met at the Opera House. 'Do you not like him?'

Adam shrugged. 'At school he was the sort of person I found hard to like or dislike, being a rather insipid sort of show off. A scholarship gained him entry, for his family were not wealthy. The majority of us took up residence at Eton courtesy of our fathers' money or influence. I was never sure whether Blackmore deemed himself superior or inferior because his father was a country parson. Mostly I avoided him.'

June was about to say that sounded rather uncharitable, but a knowing chuckle from the man at her side kept her quiet.

Adam's lips twitched at her expression. 'I expect

he had far more right than the rest of us to be at that noble establishment. He'd earned the right to be there and was definitely a studious fellow. His lowly background didn't colour my judgement of his character. There were other boys there from straitened circumstances, some of whom I still count amongst my friends. It was something else about him that rather grated on my nerves…' He shrugged. 'I never found the enthusiasm to discover exactly what it was.'

With expert handling of his perfectly matched black stallions, Adam smoothly turned the curricle and was soon proceeding back towards Hyde Park Corner. 'If he is still there, I shall introduce you. You must judge for yourself his character. And just to prove to you that I have no quarrel with him I shall invite him to my little party next week.' He grinned. 'But don't blame me if you're disappointed and find him a dull fellow.'

'I have heard William described thus.'

'William?' Adam looked genuinely surprised. 'William? Dull? Never!'

Chapter Five

'Did you enjoy your drive with my friend this afternoon?'

'I did,' June enthused with a smile. She reached across the table to slide aside the flickering candelabra so she could properly see William. In between enjoying mouthfuls of creamy asparagus chicken she told him, with a fork employed to emphasise, of the crowds they had encountered out enjoying the early spring sunshine. Suddenly her cutlery dropped back to her plate. 'You will never guess who else we saw...*and* I sought an introduction.'

'Not one of Townsend's doxies, I hope.'

June blushed at the audible irony. 'As if I would...as if *he* would,' she squeaked, embarrassed. She brought her wine glass to her mouth and sipped demurely.

William gave her an apologetic half-smile that

did nothing to lighten the gleam of amusement narrowing his vivid eyes. 'If you had asked it, I expect he would oblige you. I told you he was a villain.' He paused thoughtfully. 'Did he introduce you to his mother? I have heard that Lady Rockingham is in town, although I have not seen her.'

June shook her head sending auburn curls, burnished by candlelight, to dance about her nude shoulders. 'It was someone else. We drove past your other school friend at the entrance to Hyde Park. At the time I didn't know it was he, of course, but strangely enough a little later I found myself thinking of Gavin Blackmore and told Mr Townsend so. Round he turned, quick as you like, with great expertise for the road was busy, and took me back to be introduced.'

'And how did you like Blackmore?'

'I'm not sure I did. But then I can't say I took against him either.'

June's full, wine-ruby lips pouted with unconscious sensuality at her husband as she considered that meeting. She recalled a gentleman clear of complexion and with regular features. His colouring was rather bland: light brown hair and eyes. In all she had found Gavin Blackmore…pleasant—but, as Mr Townsend had warned her, there was nothing greatly to either like or dislike about the man. His manner had been rather enigmatic; he had postured this way and that, yet in an oddly self-conscious way that made him seem keen to conceal his nervousness. His conversation had been hardly inspired and June had been aware of Adam's mild amusement as she endeavoured to extract more from Blackmore than a blunt one-syllable response when she commented on the fine weather and the amount of people out to enjoy it.

She was too fair-minded to make any harsh judgement of his character based on one short meeting. Possibly he was shy and that accounted for his awkwardness. Yet he had not been too timid to signal he found her attractive. With a woman's intuition she knew that beneath his discreetly brief, stabbing stares lay an intention to indicate his admiration. At the time, so aware was she of his regard, that for a while she wondered if her presence was overwhelming him and making him tongue-tied. Later, driving on with Adam Townsend, such conceited presumption had made her inwardly laugh at herself.

Compared to her three beautiful sisters *she* was fairly ordinary. Rachel had always scintillated with her golden looks and character. Isabel possessed an ethereal charm that drew endless compliments. Sylvie was blessed with classical features and hair the colour of moonlight. The most June, with her slight figure, hazel eyes and reddish-blonde hair, could claim was that she had been known as the sensible Meredith girl. Of course, dear William told her time and again that she was beautiful…but then he had married her, so he would…wouldn't he?

She glanced up at the man opposite, noticing his blue eyes warm with affection as he watched her grappling with her thoughts. She shrugged away the memory of Gavin Blackmore and her silly insecurities. This was her beloved William and he loved her. 'And how was your day? Did you finalise your business?' she asked. 'What was it all about in any case?'

'Just boring legalities over my grandfather's trust.'

'Oh?' Delicate brunette brows arched questioningly. 'I thought that was all settled many years ago.'

William cut into the food on his plate. 'It is just an additional codicil regarding a fund that will be set up for any children we might have.'

June looked up slowly. 'I see,' she murmured.

'My grandfather had wanted separate provision made for my heirs.'

'That was very good of him,' June said quietly.

'Our children will thank him. He was a fine man.'

'That's not what your mother says,' June interjected wryly.

William's lips tilted a smile. 'No…and to be fair to her, she has reason to be disappointed over it all.'

'Your father has more reason. Yet he bears it all with remarkable equanimity.'

'He refused to renege on a promise for a fortune. It was a noble and gentleman-like act.'

'Indeed he is a saint and it is a shame that…'

William raised questioning eyebrows, begging his wife to conclude her statement. After a moment she obliged him.

'It is a shame that your mother doesn't seem to acknowledge the great sacrifice that he made for her. Your father must have idolised her to cede his inheritance for her sake.'

'I believe once he did. Love can make people do strange things. I often wonder if he ever regrets his decision to do the decent thing. He was just twenty-three at the time, you know.'

June nodded, wondering, as she had many times before, whether the fact that William's grandfather had left his estate to his grandson rather than to his son was the reason why Pamela, if not Alexander, was so bitter at life. William had been very young, too, when he inherited the bulk of Sir Keith Pemberton's riches…nineteen. William's father had been bequeathed just personal mementoes by the parent who had cherished him.

When Alexander told his father he had proposed marriage to Pamela Castle, Sir Keith had been keen to meet her. He wanted his daughter-in-law to be a woman worthy of his favourite boy. On first acquaintance Sir Keith was prepared to give the *little madam* the benefit of the doubt. After a few weeks socialising in Pamela's company, Sir Keith had changed his opinion. He made it clear that, if the wedding went ahead to that *common gold digger*, Alexander must forfeit his inheritance.

Despite the enormity of the financial loss, Alexander had not budged and refused to breach his promise to a humble clerk's daughter...who was distantly related to a duke.

Alexander had an older brother, little favoured by his father, for Joseph's hedonistic lifestyle had besmirched the family's good name. Joseph would take Sir Keith's title but he had had no intention of the spendthrift also having his money to squander. From the moment William was born Sir Keith doted on his flaxen-haired grandson. When, at seventy-eight, Sir Keith was advised by his physician to put his affairs in order, he knew he was never likely to know more grandsons—even supposing either of his two middle-aged daughters-in-law managed to produce any. Lawyers were summoned and William was formally bequeathed the bulk of his wealth.

June could easily understand Sir Keith Pemberton's antipathy for Pamela. June had little liking for her mother-in-law and, much as she battled to overturn that opinion, it was impossible to warm to a woman who seemed to thrive on being mean. But she had always liked William's father and respected him for showing such devotion to the woman he loved.

June's thoughts dragged to the present as she heard fingers drumming steadily on the table. She glanced at William. He looked as preoccupied as she recently had been. She changed her mind about intruding on his thoughts and instead drew one of the young servants into a chat.

William watched his wife as she graciously instructed one of the young serving girls to convey her best wishes to her mother, who had just been brought to bed with her tenth child. How difficult it must be for June to send congratulations to a poor woman burdened with another mouth to feed when she yearned to nurture her first born.

He raked fingers through his hair and prepared himself to tell his beloved wife that there was gossip he might seek a divorce. It was too ludicrous to contemplate; yet he must actually voice it. He felt fiery rage again consume him, and a shiver of sheer impotence. What could he do? If he rose to Harley's bait, the blackguard would win. Harley would relish riling him into making people think there was no smoke without fire.

When the servants had filed out, William announced quietly, 'I have something to tell you, June. It is a subject I would rather not mention, for it is bound to hurt you.'

June pushed the silver candelabra further aside. It was an unnecessary movement, for she already had an uninterrupted view of her husband. 'What is it?' she asked, half-smiling. 'Heavens! Don't look so severe or you'll frighten me half to death.'

William thrust his spine against the chair spindles. His clasped hands cupped his scalp as he gazed up at the ceiling. A short bark of laughter preceded him saying, 'It is so ludicrous I feel stupid mentioning it at all, but I want you to hear it from me rather than from malicious tongues that are already wagging.'

June felt her heart plummet to her stomach. Carefully she laced her slender fingers, then settled her hands on her lap. 'It concerns Constance Bingham, doesn't it?'

When William was tardy in replying she repeated quite shrilly, 'Doesn't it?'

'Yes.' William rose and slowly walked the length of table towards her, one languid finger skimming the shiny walnut wood.

June was mesmerised by that long caressing finger. She watched it rise to smooth her cheek as, fluidly, he crouched down by her chair.

'Look at me.'

June did as she was bid, but a stubborn shaky twist to her lips told William this was not going to be in any way easy. She was angry merely that the woman's name was again being mentioned between them.

'Is there more talk of that widow pining after you and regretting not marrying you when she had the chance? Is that it?'

'No...not exactly. A pair of idiots have been wagering that I will take her as a mistress.' William refused to let his wife flee from him and held her gently in her seat. 'There is more. A wager has also been made that I might seek a divorce to marry her.'

This time William had no need to restrain his wife. He felt her small, tense hands fall slack in his. He watched her angry flush seep away and inside he withered. But he made no attempt to soothe or cajole with pretty words. Quietly he demanded, 'Tell me you know how pathetic and ridiculous a lie it is.'

June's shocked gaze found her husband's stony features. Her tears were dammed behind fury and fright. What dominated her thoughts was the eerie recollection that recently she had wondered whether she would still be with William when he had silver hair.

William urgently shook the hands clasped in his. 'Do you not trust me, June? Do you think me capable of such behaviour?'

She shook her head wildly, her pale Titian curls flying about her fragile milky shoulders as her bodice slipped askew.

'What I want to know,' William said quietly, 'is if you would like me to run Harley and Darlington through for it? You only have to say and I shall call out both of them with every intention of striking to kill.' His voice was vibrating with repressed rage. 'Just for seeing you this upset, I would do it.'

June suddenly turned in her chair and threw her arms about her husband's neck. 'Why are they *doing* this to us?' she wailed.

'Simply to revel in the knowledge that they can,' he answered quietly. 'When I spoke to your father over it all, he said, quite wisely I thought, that contented people, such as we, rankle cynics. We must not allow them to bring us down, June.' His words were harsh with demand yet he stroked at her silky copper hair, thrusting his fingers deep into its warm mass to curve about her scalp and bring her face to his. 'I meant what I said. I will call both of them out if you want. At first I thought that we should not show those curs that they have the power to affect us. Now I'm not so sure. I hate to see you so sad.'

June managed a watery smile; again she enclosed her husband in a fierce emphatic embrace. 'Do you think I would risk my William to a cheat's tricks? Or to a gaol? That is where you would end if you were to succeed in putting those pathetic creatures out of their misery. No! I would never risk losing you. You will not call either of them out.'

She lowered her face to the handsome man gazing earnestly up at her. A soft, creamy cheek swept over the abrasive texture of his face. 'My papa has clashed with Benjamin Harley before. So has Connor. Both of them hate him. In fact, I have never heard anyone speak a good word about him. If he had no money and no influence, I'm sure he would not be received anywhere.'

A loving hand smoothed her husband's strained features. 'I trust you. I believe you. I love you and I know you love me. Harley and Darlington will simply have to find some other poor souls to torment. And Constance Bingham, I'm afraid, will just have to look elsewhere for her next husband.'

William rose to his feet, drawing June with him.

'Are we finished?' June said, looking at her unused dessert spoon. 'There is some syllabub.'

William smothered the rest of her words with a bittersweet kiss, hard as his desire, honeyed as his love. Without releasing her mouth, he swung her up into his arms, and headed for the door.

By the stairs June managed to surface long enough to choke, 'William! The servants will be back. Dessert—'

'The servants and the syllabub can wait,' her husband announced roundly as he took the first two treads in one stride. 'I'm not sure I can...'

Chapter Six

'I gather you rather like my roguish school chum.'

'He *is* very good company.'

'I'm sure. But he is a villain, June,' William emphasised with rueful gravity. 'A most charming and amusing fellow, too, I grant you. Adam springs from a very long line of fêted reprobates. The Rockinghams have long entertained society with their scandalous ways.'

'And you allow such riffraff to escort your wife? Shame on you!' June mocked with a flash of laughing eyes.

'I'm not sure why I trust a man I have not seen for so long and whom I know to be an inveterate womaniser. Yet I would vouch for him acting the perfect gentleman with you.'

'And very wise you are, for he does,' June endorsed softly. But she looked intrigued. 'Now you have whetted my appetite, you have to tell me more of his family than that,' she urged. 'Is the Fleet full of impoverished Rockinghams who have gambled away their last halfpenny? Are there mad relatives locked away in gothic turrets?' She gave a low chuckle as William's eyes narrowed in sultry humour at her teasing. 'In any case...' She playfully squeezed at William's arm and, going on her tiptoes, brought their faces close, her breath whispering warm and sweet past his lips. 'In any case,' she softly echoed, 'the Merediths are able to boast a scandal or two of their own. We are not fazed by notoriety,' she proudly announced.

A discreet caress welcomed the seductive pressure of her hip against his. 'True. But your sisters' youthful misdemeanours are as nothing compared to some of the Rockingham sons' sins.'

'Were some of those men pirates? Smugglers?' June was only half-jesting, for she was genuinely interested in finding out more about their host's intriguing history.

'All of that and more, I suspect,' William told her. 'I recall spending one school holiday with Adam when I was about fourteen. We spent an entire afternoon exploring the eaves' rooms of Rockingham Hall—' He broke off to digress. 'We were trespassing. All those rooms were out of bounds. The Hall is a draughty old medieval house and the thing I remember most about it is that it seemed an endless maze of icy corridors.' He resumed his tale. 'Anyway, in one locked room—of which Adam expertly picked the lock—there was a portrait of a barbarous-looking cove with lengthy black hair and a monkey crouched on his shoulder. Adam asked his father about him and was thrashed for revealing his intrusion and his inquisitiveness. Adam, being Adam, was undeterred by that and persevered with his investigations into the man's history. When back at school, he told me that he was a disgraced Earl who had turned to life as a privateer and had got rich again from sugar plantations. He was very bad even by Rockingham standards.'

June looked fascinated, but murmured, 'Perhaps they all have improved since. I expect the portrait might have been some centuries old.'

'It was relatively recently that his great-grandfather was gadding about in caves in West Wycombe, or so rumour has it.'

June's eyes widened. 'No! Really?' Her lucid amber eyes slipped sideways to target their handsome host and she cocked her head to one side. She had heard whispers of the tales of the Hell Fire Club, whose wicked members engaged in unspeakable acts whilst dressed in ceremonial robes. A shocked laugh bubbled in her throat. 'I'm sure Mr Townsend is much too civilised for such tomfoolery. I might not know him as well as you, but even I can see he would not look well in monk's garb.'

William chuckled. 'What a pity! No orgy tonight!' A heavy-lidded suggestive look preceded him saying, 'We could create our own diversion later.' As his wife prettily blushed, and gave his arm a punitive bang, William cast a discreet eye over her shapely curves.

June was dressed in quite demure style, as ever. She rarely opted for daring fashions that left little to the imagination. But for him, she looked delectable and desirable, however modestly she was garbed. He knew other men must find her as attractive as he did. Adam Townsend had told him more than once he was lucky in his choice of wife. June had a beauty of countenance and nature that made her seem alluring yet vulnerable. It made him—and he suspected other men who escorted her—want to act the hero protecting her. William took a glance to the left at his old friend.

Adam and his mother, Eleanor, Lady Rockingham, were greeting guests at the stately entrance to the vast ballroom of Number 20 Upper Brook Street.

William assessed his wife's suave admirer, noting his muscular stature and dark thick hair, in the manner of a man measuring a rival. Luckily he was not a possessive man. He never had been of a jealous disposition. When Constance Palmer had jilted him in favour of a better catch, everyone praised him for being stoic and mature beyond his years. William could recall feeling a little guilty at the unwanted praise and sympathy. It had seemed to him to be churlish to point out that Constance had never captured his heart and soul and her defection was more inconvenient than inconsolable.

But June had his heart and soul and he wondered how her defection might have affected him. He imagined stoicism would have swiftly deserted him along with his lauded maturity. Losing her might have seen him howling like a baby. He brought his odd musings to an abrupt halt and frowned at his shoes. It had never before occurred to him to analyse his reaction to an imaginary separation from the woman he loved. Why would he? It would never happen.

'It is a shame the Marquess of Rockingham is ailing. I should have liked to meet him,' June hissed in a whisper. Her eyes continued to watch elegant ladies and gentlemen proceeding with much aplomb over polished wooden boards to mark territory in which to preen and peruse.

'I have not seen Adam in an age and he has certainly not broadcast the fact that his father has deteriorated mentally.' William grimaced as he said, 'He and his father have never got on. He dotes on his mother, however. I like her. She always made me welcome when I went to stay during school holidays.'

'Family feuds are horrible,' June said significantly. 'Was his father cruel to him? You said he beat Adam when he discovered that pirate's portrait.'

'I think a polarity of personalities causes them to be constantly at odds. I remember his father being a bit of a puritan. Despite his money and influence, the old Marquess has never cared to enjoy himself. That cannot be said for his heir. Adam was always very aware of life's pleasures. A pure Rockingham through and through—'

'Oh, look!' June interrupted and shook William's arm. 'Here is your other school friend. Mr Blackmore is just arrived.' June recognised him immediately, for it was only a week or so ago that Adam had stopped his curricle by the Park gates to introduce them.

William was staring at the gentleman being welcomed by Lady Rockingham and her son. 'By Heaven, it is him! Perhaps we ought go and talk to him.' He turned to June as Gavin Blackmore proceeded, alone, into the room. 'He looks a little forlorn over there on his own.'

As they picked a path through scented air and silk and satin to where Mr Blackmore stood—so

close to a potted palm it seemed he intended shrinking behind it—June reminded herself how lucky she
was to be married to a man of such philanthropy
and sensitivity that he would immediately wish to
make welcome an old acquaintance he had not seen
in more than a decade.

'I always envied your husband, you know, Mrs
Pemberton, even at school and years before I
learned what a beautiful wife he has.'

June's cheeks bloomed rosily at the compliment
and she smiled sweetly at Gavin Blackmore, but her
eyes again scanned the room for William. It had
been some while since he left her side. Summoned
by his mother's urgently crooked and waggling finger, he had excused himself and strolled off, sigh-
ing, to see what it was she wanted.

June's sparkling amber eyes again alighted on the
man at her side. In her husband's absence she was
quite content to keep him company. Mr Blackmore
might not be quite as tall or dark as Adam Townsend but, now she had had a chance to study him
more closely, she thought his mild looks and diffident manner rather appealing. She had been correct in supposing that at their first meeting he might
have been endeavouring to conceal his shy nature
with a show of confidence.

This evening he seemed less inclined to try to

impress. He also seemed overawed by his surroundings and constantly darted glances up and down and around and about at the magnificent appointments in Adam Townsend's mansion.

June attempted to put him at ease by reminding him of the one thing at which she knew he had excelled. 'I have been told that you were an exemplary student at Eton. No doubt there were many at school who envied you your intellect.'

'Oh!' Gavin twisted a smile and seemed a little disconcerted. 'I gather you have been informed that I was rather the poor boy at school. Did your husband tell you I scraped a place at Eton from a scholarship, or was it Townsend's doing?'

'It was Mr Townsend…I should say…his lordship's doing, for I keep forgetting that he is so seriously lofty. William says he has never much bothered about using his courtesy title. I never realised he was the Earl of Malvern.' A little smile followed that. 'And he was complimentary about your achievements.'

'Was he?' A slight sourness honed Gavin's tone and tugged down one side of his lips. 'I don't recall ever receiving a kind word from him at Eton. But he gave me a beating. And oh, yes, he is exceedingly lofty. He was always keen to keep lesser mortals firmly in their place, when he noticed they existed. I was astonished to receive an invitation to his soirée tonight. Or perhaps that was your doing. Townsend always liked to impress the ladies.' He gave June a boyish smile. 'I'm not complaining. I'm thanking you, for it is indeed a most lavish affair. Did you persuade him to invite me?'

June murmured, a trifle abashed, 'No…' but she knew her cheeks had tinted with guilt. Adam's intention in inviting this man to his party had been, so he had said, to prove to her that he harboured no animosity towards him. Her eyes strayed to where their splendidly sophisticated host was grouped with some ladies and gentlemen. He was a villain, she reminded herself. Even her William had warned her of that. But she baulked at believing him a pompous bully. 'I'm sorry to hear that Lord Malvern beat you.' She said no more for she didn't want to be drawn into blaming or championing their host. Neither did she want to be seen to be inquisitive enough to pry for further details.

Gavin's careless shrug demonstrated his willingness to let bygones be bygones. 'It was nothing, of course. Boys will be boys. Thrashings, boasts, all are just part of being at boarding school. It is a most hierarchical life.' A suitably brave smile accompanied the explanation. 'Of course, my griping might have a little to do with the fact that I was…still am…exceedingly jealous of him. Who would not be? He has everything.' A small gesture indicated the opulence all around. 'Townsend always had everything any man could want including, as I said, a most successful way with the ladies.'

'You said you envied William, too. Did my husband also have a successful way with the ladies?' June enquired with a teasing smile.

'Well, I'm sure such a personable man had his admirers, but I did not witness anything...anything excessive,' was Gavin's diplomatic answer. 'Your husband was an all-round good chap. I think everyone—even Townsend—envied William. He was incredibly popular, clever, a fine sportsman. It is no surprise to me that a man so blessed managed to persuade a lovely, charming lady to marry him.'

As June again coloured at his praise, Gavin looked momentarily apologetic. 'It is not insincere flattery. I mean what I say.' He paused, moved awkwardly from foot to foot. 'I am afraid I made rather a fool of myself when we were first introduced at the Park. I must have seemed to you a witless idiot to act so tongue-tied. The truth is, you rather overwhelmed me. But then I expect you have that effect on other gentlemen.' He gave a little nervous rub to the bridge of his nose. 'I'm sorry if my regard makes you feel uncomfortable.'

June touched his arm lightly, reassuringly. 'It does not. It is kind of you to be lavish with your compliments.'

June looked at Gavin's tense, proud features. She guessed it was in his nature to be bluff; no doubt he would feel rather out of place in such sophisticated company as this. Possibly he regretted coming at all and having revealed so much of himself to a woman he barely knew. June sensed a sudden surge of empathy. She was no stranger to feeling envious. Did she not sometimes consider herself unfortunately plain in comparison to her startlingly beautiful siblings? Had she not felt resentful and self-pitying on learning that Rachel was to soon have another baby? She could sense this gentleman attempting to repress similar emotions to those that had recently bedevilled her.

'Envy can stimulate us to try harder…or it can be a most destructive emotion,' she softly said. 'Sometimes it is difficult not to be angry when something you believe you deserve…something dear to your heart…is denied you. Life can be unfair in how it distributes its bounty.'

Gavin Blackmore gave her a grateful smile. 'You are perceptive as well as charming, Mrs Pemberton. But not too perceptive, I hope, for I sometimes worry I can be a bore and I should like your good opinion.'

'And you have it. I do not at all think you boring. I have enjoyed our chat.' June glanced about and said, 'I suppose I ought go and rescue William from his mother. She can be quite a…tenacious lady.'

'I think William has managed to extricate himself,' Gavin said with a flicker of a smile. 'I'm sure I saw him go outside…just a moment ago.'

June felt her insides tighten, for something about Gavin's attitude made her sure he immediately regretted telling her so. She sensed he also did not want to disclose whether William had stepped alone on to the terrace.

'I must not keep you from your husband or take up any more of your time.' He executed a polite bow for her.

Having said farewell, June turned away to begin her search for William. After a few steps she pivoted back in a rustle of cream silk to see Mr Blackmore had not moved and was watching her. 'Did my husband go alone on to the terrace?'

Gavin cleared his throat, frowned over her head as he gripped his hands behind his back. 'I believe he was with Lady Bingham…and some others,' he tacked on quickly, perhaps too quickly.

A constrained smile met that news. June tilted her chin. Following the latest outrageous gossip, perhaps her perfect husband ought to know he was acting rather rashly by being seen again in the company of that woman. June strove to sound insouciant as she asked, 'Do you know Lady Bingham,

Mr Blackmore?' She came towards him again as she spoke.

'We come from the same part of the country…Devonshire. Not that I socialised much with Lady Bingham and her late husband. I might have been lucky enough to secure an education at Eton, but even my father's best efforts could never gain me an entrée into such circles.'

'Constance and William were once engaged, you know. Then she chose to marry Lord Bingham instead.'

'Yes, I knew of that. I'm sure William is glad that it all turned out for the best. I'm sure, too, he would never knowingly snub anyone, however tempted he might be to do so.'

'I gather from your tactful response that you are aware of gossip concerning my husband and Lady Bingham. You need not fear embarrassing me. William and I have dismissed it. We will never let malice ruin our happiness.'

Gavin gave a relieved sigh. 'Very sensible too! I feared that I might inadvertently disclose what I knew and that might make you angry—'

He suddenly fell silent and frowned, making June suspect he had been about to say more.

'I must go now. I did not mean to stay long. But I am glad to have again had an opportunity to talk to you, Mrs Pemberton.'

June put a light hand on his arm. 'Must you go so soon?' There was just a suspicion that he had been about to disclose something else…something, she sensed, that she didn't know.

With a look that told her how easily she could sway him, Gavin drew June slightly behind the potted palm he had sought as company when first he arrived alone. 'Perhaps you would do me the honour of allowing me to take you for a drive one afternoon…with your husband's permission, of course. I shall call next week, if that is convenient.'

Having gained a small nod in response, he bowed briefly and was soon striding away.

'You seemed very deep in conversation with my old friend. I was loath to interrupt. His manners are still sadly lacking. He has dashed past me with barely a farewell. Have you given him a well-deserved set-down?'

June turned to see Adam Townsend smiling at her. He looked outrageously handsome in his excellently tailored dark clothes. 'I hope I have not,' she said, struggling to find a smile. 'I think Mr Blackmore simply felt a little…left out of it. I have the impression he knows few people here this evening.'

Adam's shrug was indifferent. 'Where is William? I was looking for him earlier.'

'So was I,' June announced a trifle tartly. 'I believe he might be outside on the terrace.'

Adam gallantly proffered an arm. 'Let us see, then, if we can find him.'

After a stroll in the chill moonlight and no sign of William, they returned to the supper room, and it was there that William found them. He drew his wife away from Adam, who relinquished her with a theatrically regretful sigh.

It took but one long look for William to sense his wife was angry and hurt. 'What is it?' he demanded with a fierce look at their urbane host some way in the distance now. 'I saw you come in from the terrace with him. Has Townsend at last disgraced himself with you?'

'Of course not!' June looked up into her husband's face. 'Have *you* disgraced yourself…or me? Did you accompany Lady Bingham outside a little while ago?' she accused bluntly.

William's face darkened. 'I went to the terrace with Isabel and Etienne. Constance Bingham, I believe, was right behind us with several other people. There was talk of a shooting star having been seen in the night sky. In all, twenty or more people ventured outside, hoping for a glimpse of it. It grew so crowded that I was soon again inside and looking for you.'

June stared up at him, blatant angry suspicion still firing her golden eyes.

William suddenly captured her soft arm in a firm grip and drew his wife close to a marble pillar so they could talk more privately. 'When we spoke of this the other evening, I thought we had agreed to ignore the gossip and act normally. It would have seemed exceedingly odd had I turned around and fled as soon as I noticed that Constance Bingham was in the vicinity. I thought you had told me you trusted me. Is that not so? Am I going to have to beg permission to go out, and justify my every movement to you, June? Do you want a husband or a lap dog that will never leave your side? If you wish it, I will be your pet, you only have to say, my dear.' He struck a hand over her head to lounge against the pillar. Only a keen observer would have seen his knuckles whiter than the marble they gripped as he strove to shield their discord from prying eyes. 'Is there ever to be any trust and harmony again in this marriage?' The reprimand was blasted through teeth that looked set perilously tight.

Over one of his broad, bunched shoulders, the pale oval of June's face was just visible. Her complexion was stark white against the black cloth of his jacket. Her teary tawny gaze focussed on a woman who was watching them…watching them intently. Aware of June's eyes on her, Constance Bingham tilted her head slightly to one side then with triumph flaring in her eyes she turned away.

Chapter Seven

'We will pack today and leave for Grove House tomorrow.'

The bluntly delivered instruction brought up June's chin. Over her raised coffee cup she challenged her husband's edict with brilliant tiger eyes.

So far this morning they had breakfasted in total silence. A little over ten hours earlier they had returned from Adam Townsend's ball in much the same icy atmosphere. June knew that a depressing pattern was emerging in their lives. Invariably they set out happily in the evening to socialise with friends and family, yet returned home in low spirits with a wall of tension between them.

Yesterday at midnight, they had wordlessly entered their cosy house in Mayfair and stiffly gone their separate ways. June had headed for the stairs and her chamber. Her husband had stridden immediately towards his study. The sound of the door slamming shut had disclosed his unabated frustration. She had no need to move closer to that room to know the brandy decanter would be in use. Nevertheless, with a sad sigh she had retraced her steps down the stairs with the intention of offering an olive branch. They could then at least retire for the evening with the prospect of some sleep, if no raw, healing passion.

In the event as she came closer to William's study, what she heard was a string of muttered oaths pouring forth. She had returned to the stairs and to the knowledge that it would be a very long and sombre night.

When the door to William's chamber was quietly shut in the small chill hours of the morning she was still restless. Now as she discreetly studied him, she noticed a pinch of tiredness to his features and dark beneath his eyes. She guessed he had found no more repose than had she last night. But one thing she *had* decided upon while she tossed and turned, feeling one moment entirely blameless, the next hideously at fault, was that she was glad she was close to her parents and her sisters. Never before had she realised just how much she appreciated their comfort and support.

'I have no wish to go to Essex. I want to stay by my family in London. I thought we had agreed that the malicious people who wish to torment us would not drive us into hiding.'

'So did I,' her husband said quietly. 'But after last night I am prepared to admit defeat on this. I have no intention of enduring any more of your sulks and accusations. We must leave London.'

'I have not been sulking!' June snapped. 'And I think I was perfectly entitled to enquire whether you had been seen in the company of Constance Bingham. Considering what gossip has been bandied about, it was rather…rather ill advised of you to go outside with her, even if other people were also present.'

William gained his feet so abruptly his chair clattered on to its back. His eyes flicked distractedly as though in search of something on which he might vent his anger. Five fingers dug trenches straight through his thick fair hair. 'Instruct your maid, Verity, and choose a few other servants you would like to accompany you to Grove House. The arrangements have already been made. I want to leave by ten in the morning.'

June smartly set down her cup on to its saucer. 'And *I* have no intention of being carted off to the country. Are you going to abandon me there and return at your leisure so you may do as you please without me witnessing it and thus nagging you?'

William slanted June a fierce low-lidded look.

'Do you really think that is what I would do?' When she refused to answer him, he bellowed, *'Do you?'*

'No.' Her hands flew to cover her face. 'I'm sorry. That was a stupid thing to say. It seems so easy lately to say stupid things.' When her husband made no attempt to placate her with words or touches—and how she yearned that he would cuddle her—she proudly raised her head. With a subtle touch the tears weighting her lashes were dashed off. 'I want to stay here with my family. I need to see my sisters…my parents. Can't you understand that I need to be close to people who care for me whilst we deal with this awful situation?'

After a silence that throbbed, seemed laden with tension, William enquired with cool politeness, 'Do I not care for you then?'

June gripped the table with both her small hands. 'I hope so…I *do* hope so. But just lately I should like a little more hard proof of your feelings for me, William.'

William's cold blue gaze was unwavering, yet a glimmer of amusement was far back in eyes that were becoming sleepy.

June flushed and looked at her breakfast plate as it dawned on her how indelicately she had phrased her needs. She thus missed the smile softening the hard edge to her husband's mouth.

Slowly William withdrew his watch and studied it. 'Well, I have fifteen minutes to spare before I'm due at my attorney's…'

June shoved away from the table and was, in a whisper of sprigged muslin, halfway to the door when he caught her and whirled her about. Off balance, she tipped straight into his welcoming arms.

'Just a joke…I've all morning…all day…all the time in the world for you. You must know that.'

'There is other proof, you know!' June didn't persist for long with her feeble attempts to extricate herself. She allowed him to hold her, for moments before she had pined for this comfort. Half-heartedly she scolded, 'There are other ways you might show me you care; that you love me and cherish me and…'

'I know,' her husband answered softly, a finger tracing a curve of her cheek, soothing her pique. 'But that way seems to work best, and I confess I like it. Don't you?' He gave one side of her mutinously strict lips a soft kiss. When she refused to respond he enclosed her tightly and rested his chin atop a crown of glossy Titian hair. 'How then shall I show you I love you?'

Indifferent shoulders lifted, then slumped within his embrace.

'Shall I pen Constance Bingham a note informing her she is a hag and dispatch it forthwith?'

June's choke of laughter and frantic shake of her

head had him moving loving hands over her slender spine, drawing her imperceptibly closer to undeniable proof of his desire for her. 'I've already offered to meet Harley and Darlington at dawn and risk life and limb for you in a misty glade.'

June tipped up her head, looked into the warm cerulean gaze that roved her face. She was already won over. She yearned for the touch of his mouth on hers, the cool sleek sensation of his velvet skin moving on her body.

'I know what you'd like: the diamond rope bangle we saw when out last week. I noticed you linger by it.'

Swiftly June put up a finger, placed it over her husband's lips.

William kissed it, turned his face so the soft digit smoothed his cheek. 'No? You don't want it? I know you'd rather I made your arms tired with the weight of our baby but it seems, much as I love you, that gift is beyond me…'

June wound her arms tightly about his neck. Abruptly she released him and was soon by the door. 'In five minutes come upstairs. More than anything I long for such proof of our love and it is not beyond you…or me.'

'It is an outrage too far! Are you certain?' Edgar Meredith's bluish lips virtually disappeared, so grimly were they set.

Etienne looked to Connor to respond to their father-in-law's hoarse demand. Connor sighed and
nodded his head. 'We both heard what was said.'

Edgar dragged off his spectacles and, in shock,
let them carelessly clatter to his desk. A mottled
hand covered his eyes, massaged wearily as though
to ease away strain beneath straggly brows. Eventually he said, 'Do you think this is yet more of
Harley's mischief?'

'I've no idea,' Connor told him truthfully.
'White's was crowded, but I don't think Harley or
Darlington were there. The conversation we overheard was not malicious. It was just a bit of ribald
banter between a few young bucks. They looked to
be still wet behind the ears. When they noticed we
seemed annoyed at what they were saying, they
made a swift exit.'

Etienne sighed pessimistically before joining in
the conversation. 'William won't take this as phil-
osophically as he has the other rumours, that's for
sure.'

'How do you think my June will react to it all?'
Edgar exploded. 'She and William are looking
more and more as though a rift is opening wide
between them. They quit Townsend's party the
other evening looking morose. It is being noticed
that all is not well. More than once recently I've

had to deflect impertinent inquisitiveness on the state of their marriage.' Edgar frowned at his sons-in-law. 'Are Rachel and Isabel aware of this? Have you yet told them? I know they will not want to hurt their sister but they will not want to conceal anything so vital from June either. They would hate her to hear it when out and unprepared for such devastating news.'

Etienne and Connor, with a simultaneous shake of dark heads, denied having had an opportunity to tell their wives about this episode. Edgar scooped up his spectacles and nodded in meagre satisfaction. 'Well, that gives us a little time I suppose to sort out what must be done. And I fear that *we* must do it, for even a fellow as placid as William will feel it his duty to call out whomever has so maligned him. And he might shoot to kill the devil.'

Etienne frowned. 'There is something else that occurs to me; with respect, sir, we are all men of the world. Do you think that perhaps we ought to speak urgently to William before we act, in case there is a possibility a grain of truth exists in it? William and Constance Palmer were betrothed for some months, after all…'

Edgar stared, and as the full implication hit him, he squeezed shut his eyes and gulped back the outrage that had been on the point of blasting forth from his puckered lips. What did emerge eventually was a muted oath followed by, 'I must be older than I think, for I admit that had not occurred to me. And yet it should have, for now I ponder on it, that infernal woman did jilt William, then go on to marry Charlie Bingham with indecent haste.'

'Supposing it to be true…do you think perhaps the lady might bizarrely feel she has a valid claim on William? Has she got a hand in it all?' Connor elevated his shoulders, indicating it was no more than a suggestion.

'Bingham's first wife died childless…' Edgar muttered almost to himself.

'There were rumours before that, which seemed unfounded, of course, when he married for the second time and started his family,' Etienne added cautiously.

The three men looked at one another. Edgar slowly sank into his desk chair. 'If proven, what an awful irony it would be! Please God it is not true, for I fear it might transform those other lies to truth. Divorce! It ought not be uttered in the same breath as June's name, yet it no longer seems outlandish. Indeed, in my opinion it would be unendurable for June to stay with William should it be proven he has sired Constance Bingham's daughter.'

'I am going to be on my best behaviour this afternoon and say nothing that might easily embarrass you.'

'What makes you think I am easily embarrassed?'

Gavin Blackmore slid June a teasing grin. 'You blush every time I compliment you.'

June put a pale hand to a pink cheek. 'I have a naturally high colour,' she fibbed on a shy smile.

'You have rosebuds in your cheeks. And I am glad that I am able to put them there, for it suits you very much.'

'You promised to be on your best behaviour this afternoon.' The reprimand was followed by a coy cluck of the tongue. 'I'm not sure such praise lavished on a happily married lady *is* good behaviour, sir.'

Gavin let the reins slacken in his fingers and the modest equipage he had hired to take them for an afternoon drive slowed to a sedate pace. 'I think you know I would rather die than offend you.' The words were vibrant with sincerity and a look mingling apology and adoration bathed her face.

'I'm not at all offended,' June reassured lightly and, after a smile, turned her head. During the following quiet minutes they spent inspecting passing landmarks, June was aware of Gavin taking sidelong peeks at her profile.

It was the third time they had taken an afternoon drive together while William's commerce kept him closeted with his men of business in Cheapside. Now June had got to know Gavin Blackmore better, she had discovered he could be amiable and amusing. He was a good mimic and satirist and several prominent figures had, earlier in the week, been wittily subjected to the sharp side of his tongue. She had, between chuckles, scolded him and warned that he risked being incarcerated for sedition if he carried on so.

Assuming a humble pose, he had promised to desist and changed the subject. And the subject he again settled on was her. The constancy of his compliments was quite alarming, for it was unlike the practised gallantry that Adam Townsend casually bestowed on her…and she imagined many other ladies of his acquaintance. Yet June was not displeased by Gavin's attention. It was flattering for the *sensible* Meredith girl to be the object of such ardent admiration from a man who, despite his mature years, was obviously a novice at flirtation.

June was unpractised in such arts, too. She had never before had much opportunity to test her feminine wiles for she had married young, to her one and only love. And she was sure she didn't regret any of it…

At her débutante ball William had appeared to notice her at the same moment she saw him. An unspoken bond seemed to forge between them and, shortly after she wished he would, he had come to her side. They had danced together perfectly, talked together as though long acquainted. Before the evening was over she had known with a sense of serenity that he would offer for her in the morning. Equally, she knew she would readily consent to be his wife. They were engaged before her first season had got properly under way. She had never before pondered on whether she missed the thrill of enticing men to notice her, whether she regretted acting mature for her years when barely out of her teens. For, eager to please her acid-tongued mother-in-law, June had conducted herself with modesty and decorum from the outset.

'I feel we are becoming friends, so I hope you will not mind me saying that sometimes you look a little…wistful. I hope it is not due to spiteful people, for I am quite afraid you will choose to escape to your retreat in the Essex countryside. I hope you do not. I shall miss your company and our little outings.'

'William and I will not be driven from our home by those nasty tattle-mongers,' June confidently told him.

At Adam Townsend's ball she had had an instinct Gavin was nervous of inadvertently revealing something sensational. June had decided not to

probe but heed her husband's quiet wisdom, bestowed after their passionate reconciliation earlier
in the week. 'Let us avoid even thinking of any of
it, sweetheart,' he had impressed on her. 'In that
way we will certainly frustrate those fools who
think they can torment us.'

With a secret smile, June thought further about
that delightful time; she thought of how very easily
she had persuaded her husband to change his mind
about going to Essex. He had groaned as she covered his face with tiny kisses and pressed home her
suit, but then within a pleasurable while she had
groaned too, so loud he had had to stop her with
his kiss covering her mouth and with a whispered
scold that she would startle the servants…

As she felt her face flame with her reminiscences
she brightly blurted out those other valid reasons
for staying in London. 'My family is in town for
the season. We must make the most of our times
together. Soon Rachel will be returning to Ireland,
and Isabel will go to Suffolk. If Sylvie does not
attract a husband—and Heaven knows I don't believe she is even ready for one—she and my parents
will journey back to Windrush, my childhood home
in Hertfordshire. We all adore Windrush. We spent
some very happy childhood days there.' She gave
Gavin a smile. 'Enough of me and mine…you have
told me nothing about your family.'

Immediately he averted his face as though she had mentioned something disconcerting.

June persevered. 'Do you have brothers or sisters?' In response June received a brief nod. 'I believe it was Adam Townsend who informed me your father was a clergyman. You must have spent your early years in a rural vicarage; or perhaps you lived in a town in Devon…'

'I lived at The Rookery, which was the parsonage in Maybury village. I wish I could say they were happy days,' he informed quietly. 'My mother died in childbed when my younger sister was born. My father was a cold and brutal man who would preach damnation at us with the same zeal he addressed his congregation.' He gave June a taut smile. 'I am sorry but I have no pretty pastoral tales of romping through meadows or of sunny days angling in a clear stream. My father found chores for us every day. His favourite quote was, "The devil makes work for idle hands". Mostly my childhood was unremittingly bleak.' Gavin slid a wary glance at June as though ready to flinch at her disgust at such unsavoury reminiscence.

June's expression radiated sympathy as her eyes implored him to continue.

'My father treated my sister little better than he did me. In truth, I think he blamed Bethany for our mother's demise. Time and again I shielded her from a beating by taking the blame for some prank of hers.'

Gavin suddenly whipped the horses into faster pace, indicating he hoped he had said enough to satisfy June's curiosity.

'You must have missed your mother dreadfully. Were you still quite young when she died?'

Gavin looked resigned to her perseverance. He reined in the horses to a more sedate pace. 'I was seven. And, yes, I missed her dreadfully. When my father was remarried to his housekeeper—I think he married her simply to save himself her remuneration—things were worse for us. In her new position she became as harsh as he. I think she hoped to have children of her own and usurp us. But fortunately we were not burdened with any of their offspring. Bethany and I had no step-siblings to contend with.'

'Does Bethany still live in Devonshire with your father and stepmother?'

'No. They are both dead, and good riddance to that. I know it is a terrible thing to say about one's parent, but my father showed us no love and little attention, unless it was to bend us to his will.' He paused for a moment and at last turned his head to look at her. 'Bethany has endured a hard and cruel life. I have helped her as much as I can, but I am not a wealthy man. Bethany was married quite young to a man who was not worthy of her. I think she accepted the first offer of marriage that came her way simply to escape from the hell that was our home. My stepmother was delighted to be rid of her. My brother-in-law had a small importing business in Bristol. But Bethany, bless her, leapt from the frying pan into the fire with that cur. He regularly beat her and kept her short of food and other necessities. She absconded as far away as possible with what funds she had. She is here in London, but in grave trouble. One of the reasons I came here was to try and help her. I do what I can.'

June dropped her eyes from his. A light hand rested on his sleeve. 'I feel very sad for you. I wish I had not mentioned my happy childhood. It must be galling to have had to listen to my speaking of Windrush.'

'I enjoy hearing of your family. Please don't pity me; I could not stand that…not from you. I have been pitied as the poor boy all my life.'

'You mean at Eton?'

Gavin nodded.

'At least your father did one good thing for you and helped you gain a scholarship.'

Gavin's top lip curled in a sneer. 'He did it for himself, not for me. He wanted to associate with distinguished families in the neighbourhood. He hoped to gain an introduction to the wealthy and

influential. My stepmother was scathing of my inability to make many friends at school. No rich
lord's son ever invited me to stay with them during
school holidays.'

'But I think…I guess from what you have said
that you are close to your sister. I imagine you are
a comfort to each other,' June said carefully.

Gavin nodded and his tight lips softened. 'Yes,
Bethany and I are close and a comfort to each
other.'

'I should like to meet her. As she lives in London, perhaps we could pay her a visit. It is still
early.'

Gavin gave June a lengthy look in which he appeared to be considering her request. 'That is very
good of you. I should like you to meet, but I'm not
sure you would still want to should you know
where she presently resides.'

June masked her incipient alarm as she calmly
enquired, 'Is she now living in a different sort of
rookery? Is she in a slum?'

'No, she's in a gaol,' was Gavin's bleak response.

Chapter Eight

'In a gaol?'

The horrified demand was barely audible and elicited from Gavin a rueful smile. 'I am sorry if I have shocked you with tales of my abysmal family's woes, Mrs Pemberton.'

'You have not shocked me…' June protested, then sighed in defeat. 'I own I am shocked, and very sorry that your sister has suffered such trials and tribulations. You, too, it seems, have not had an easy life,' she added in a tone resonant with sympathy.

'Bethany has suffered far harsher treatment than have I. She is in a debtor's prison. I expect you have heard of the Fleet. Please God you never see its accommodation, or come within range of its stench.'

June gazed at the rigid profile presented to her.

Gavin simply kept his eyes on the road and the horses trotting. 'Is it not possible to gain your sister's release from that awful place?'

'I could never find enough to pay what she owes. As I have said, I am not a wealthy man. I have bribed her gaoler to make sure she has at least some edible food each day. And he brings her washing water. I have tried to scrape her a few comforts—' He broke off to bark harshly, 'Comforts! How stupid to use such a word. Of course a human being ought be entitled to such basic necessities.'

'I should like to help…'

It seemed Gavin did not hear June's offer, for he continued in a tone of repressed rage, 'Bethany has fled from that monster she married only to be hounded by the cost of freedom. If only she had waited just a little while longer, I would have made arrangements for her escape. I told her that. But she can be impulsive. She hired a rig and a driver and was charged an extortionate price. Then, when in the city, she needed somewhere to stay and the friend she thought she had found turned out to be no friend at all but a procuress. Bethany immediately sought her own lodgings elsewhere, but she has never been able to haggle. She would always give over whatever amount was asked of her, fearing her dignity would be compromised should she tender a shilling less.'

He shook his head in despair. 'What dignity has she now? She weeps away the day and night. By the time I had caught up with her the duns were hot on her heels. Within a few days they had brought her up before the magistrate. If only I could pay off her debts!' His fist was slammed in frustration against a solid thigh, and June noticed his lips tighten against his teeth.

'You should not have hired this rig to take me for a drive. Not today or earlier in the week. That expense would have been better spent helping your sister.'

Gavin acknowledged that truth with a short, uneasy laugh. 'I do not regret indulging my desire to see you. I have enjoyed our drives. There! I confess I am a selfish beast. Bethany, of course, tells me I do too much for her. She scolds me for wasting my money on bribes given to a pig of a gaoler. I'm quite sure the oaf could do more for her for what I pay him.'

'It must be dreadful for her!' June cried softly. 'I shall speak to William and…'

'I beg you will not do that.' The demand was gritted out in such a harsh and authoritative tone that it startled June into staring at him.

Quickly Gavin steered the rig to the side of the road and brought it to a halt. He turned to June and his expression was calm and yet implacable. Gently he took her hands into his. 'I thank you very much for the offer to speak to your husband on my account, Mrs Pemberton, but I cannot allow it. Indeed, I would be grateful if you would not repeat what I have told you today to anyone at all. I hope I am not a proud man, but neither do I want charity or pity from my peers. I had my fill of being patronised in my youth when sent to school with people who considered me an upstart. I shall strive to bring this right for Bethany, and I know I can trust you to keep what I have told you to yourself.' He suddenly smiled. 'I am grateful to you for your condolences, and for allowing me to unburden myself. I feel quite isolated at times and it is nice to have a friend to talk to.'

June squeezed his fingers, then gently extricated her own. Suddenly her problems seemed rather trivial. Malicious gossip was unpleasant, but it could not injure her physically. She guessed that Bethany Blackmore was younger than herself and in her tender years she had endured much hurt and hardship. 'Has Bethany enough clothing to keep her warm? It has been quite bitter cold at night. I imagine the damp in such a place must seep into one's bones.'

Gavin dropped his chin. 'I brought her a blanket and a warm shawl, but one of the other women stole those.' He choked a laugh that petered out and was followed by a rueful shake of the head. 'My Bethany is an intrepid character. She attempted to get her things back, of course, and has quite a shiner to show she has no talent as a pugilist.'

June unwound the soft silky scarf from her neck and drew off her calf-leather gloves. 'You must take these to her. I insist!' she ordered when he made to immediately protest. 'If she wears them at all times no one will be able to steal them. I shall get more for her. Warm stockings and…underthings…' She barely blushed as she mentioned the unmentionables.

Gavin carefully, reverently, folded the items that she had given him. 'Thank you.'

June said brightly, 'And next time we go for a ride we must use my transport. Perhaps later this week we should meet again. I shall bring those garments for your sister, and you must tell me how she fares.' Absorbed with the intriguing nature of it all, she added, 'Also, I shall rack my brain for a money-making scheme to help pay off the debts.'

'I have spent many a sleepless night doing just that. There is nothing I can think of other than to be lucky at the tables, or perhaps to put a wager on a boxing match or the Epsom races.' Gavin sighed dolefully. 'But such luck has always eluded me. Perhaps you might attract good fortune…'

'It is time for me to return home, and I *shall*

speak to William.' She put out a reassuring hand at Gavin's immediate disapproving frown. 'Never fear that I will disclose what you have told me. Although I do not like having secrets from William, I will respect your reasons for privacy. I shall simply quiz him over where good odds are likely to be had.'

To an observer, William's profile could have been carved from granite, so solidly was it set. Fortunately, most gentlemen in the vicinity were too engrossed in watching the card game in progress—for it seemed a sizeable fortune was about to change hands—to ponder on his stony expression. His savage fingers made to cursorily crumple the letter, recently delivered to him by a steward; instead they crisply folded it and stuffed it into a pocket.

He made a brief excuse to Adam Townsend, who slid up at him a thoughtful look before shuffling the cards in his hands and flicking them precisely about the green baize. Moments later William was making for the door of Boodle's. He was at the exit when he caught sight of his father-in-law's stocky figure striding along the pavement with the intention, it seemed, of entering the club.

Edgar Meredith quickly approached his son-in-law and, from his inferior height, glared up at William. 'Thank God you are here. Connor and Etienne have been scouring Cheapside for you; they thought you were attending to your stock portfolios this afternoon.'

'I was until recently. I have not long ago arrived here. Now I must leave.' William surfaced from the mire of anguish that dulled his mind to appreciate that his father-in-law seemed equally distracted. He wiped a hand across his chin, settling it within the comfort of thumb and forefinger. 'I hope I am wrong…but does your urgent pursuit of me mean you have already got wind of this?' William withdrew from his pocket the note he had recently received, whilst drawing his father-in-law into a convenient alcove between the buildings where they might be more secluded. Blue eyes steadily watched Edgar above the hand curled into a fist at his grimly set mouth.

Anger surged through Edgar's body and attempting to contain it made his fingers rigid. He thrust the vibrating paper back at its owner. 'Is it true?' he barked without preamble.

William beckoned curtly for his carriage and had assisted Edgar to climb in and got in himself before he uttered a reply. 'I hope to God it is not true. But if you were to ask me if it were possible…I would have to say, yes,' he admitted hoarsely. He ignored Edgar's blaspheming groan at that and again withdrew the message from his pocket. He rested it on a knee and read the few lines of boldly printed script.

I know that you have a by-blow in Devon. I expect you know who the mother is, for she makes her attentions to you plain enough. A barren wife might be insulted good and proper if this got out. Pay me a thousand guineas and nobody else will know of it. Take the money to Saul's Pawnshop in Houndsditch and never fear but it will reach me.

William had reread the note a dozen or more times when Edgar's voice penetrated the deafening fury pounding in his ears.

'The rumour is out in any case, so that blackmail note is not worth a jot. Connor and Etienne were in White's and overheard some macaronis crowing that Bingham was not the man he would have had people believe. There were rumours before that he was lacking spunk when his first wife died childless. Her four sisters had produced a score or more offspring between them.' At his son-in-law's lack of response, aside from his face tightening to a masklike stillness, Edgar added, 'Those prating dandies went on to mention you by name as the prime suspect.'

At that information William's blond head fell

back against the squabs and he stared at the carriage roof.

'Do you think that Constance Bingham has anything at all to do with this? Would she scrape the barrel in her effort to entrap you?'

A mirthless laugh scratched at William's throat. 'Hardly! It is common knowledge that Bingham left her a very rich woman. She might want a husband to replace him and she might have stupidly set her sights on me, but I don't see why she would resort to blackmail. That amount would be to her pin money. The mode of writing is hardly a lady's style, although I confess it is not difficult or novel to attempt to conceal one's true identity with such a trick.'

'Perhaps the rumours are her work, if not the note. An opportunist might simply have dashed that off, thinking to make himself a tidy profit before the tale became common knowledge.'

'If Constance, for some odd reason, now wanted to inform me that a decade ago I impregnated her, she would have found a private way to do it. Her reputation will suffer from this gossip...'

'I couldn't give a tinker's cuss what either of you suffer! It is my June *I* am concerned for. How do you think that poor innocent will fare when it comes to her hearing that you have sired a child out of wedlock? And June so desperate to be a mother herself.' Edgar had shifted forward on the seat in his agitation and his fists were wobbling close to his contorted features.

William's icy gaze quit the coach roof to cool Edgar's boiling countenance. When he spoke his voice was silky with politeness. 'I am glad that there is at least one thing on which we agree. My wife is, of course, also *my* first concern. She is to be protected at all costs from any more scandal. With that in mind I would ask you to act moderately and not create a drama where perhaps none exists. I will sort this out. There is no proof at the moment that I am guilty of any more than failing to confront Harley and Darlington sooner.'

Edgar stared, slack-jawed, at his son-in-law. This was a side of William he had not known existed. He warily eyed the blond gentleman opposite. He seemed a stranger with that ruthless set to his mouth and his blue eyes boring ferociously into a spot close to his head. Edgar had a mind to look about and see if a hole was opening in the coachworks. Edgar moistened his lips, undecided as to whether maintaining dignity required him to blast back a reprimand of his own. Inquisitiveness got the better of pride and he demanded, 'So you believe it is their doing. Will you call Harley and Darlington out?'

William shifted his eyes a fraction so they encompassed Edgar. After a moment of intense concentration he answered, 'I have some investigations to make. It is probably best to say no more than that at present.'

'I gather you are telling me to mind my own business. Don't you think your wife's father has a right to know what is going on?'

'No,' William replied tersely and, glancing through the coach window, noticed the vehicle was pulling into the kerb at Beaulieu Gardens. He had alighted in a trice and courteously helped Edgar out. With barely a farewell for his indignant father-in-law, the coach was soon again bowling down the road at a pace that looked perilous.

Pamela Pemberton was arranging some daffodils in a vase, pulling the stalks this way and that, to her dissatisfaction, when her son strode into the small salon of her neat townhouse. As always, Pamela was pleased to see her favourite child. The yellow trumpets were soon abandoned on the table and she exclaimed, 'William! Have you heard I have had a chill and come to see how I do?'

'No, ma'am,' William bluntly disabused her. 'Naturally, I am pleased to see you are not still ailing.'

'I am a mite improved.' Pamela sniffed, having hoped for a little more sympathy than she had got.

She whipped a scrap of lace-edged linen from her skirt pocket and dabbed delicately at her dry nose.

'I have come to speak to you about Constance Palmer…Lady Bingham,' William crisply corrected himself.

Pamela gawped at him, taken aback. It was not at all a topic of conversation she would have imagined her son would broach. She slanted a nervous look at the door in case Alexander might appear, for he had forbidden the woman's name to again be mentioned in his house. And Pamela was chary of displeasing her husband, for he had been uncommonly sharp with her of late.

As if on cue, Alexander strolled in and greeted his son with a clap on the back and a brisk, 'Is June not with you?' Alexander suddenly noticed his wife was quiet and her expression was stunned. An enquiring look was shot at his son.

'I apologise in advance for the unseemly nature of what I must disclose,' William commenced gravely. 'But it is as well you hear this from me. Soon there will be new gossip about Constance Bingham and me joining that already entertaining the *ton*. My brothers-in-law have overheard a conversation in one of the clubs that I sired Constance's daughter.'

'How ridiculous!' Pamela burst out on a scathing laugh. The silver salts bottle she had withdrawn as a precaution was airily wafted beneath her nostrils before being dropped back in her pocket. 'How could it be true? You were no more than betrothed to her…' Her voice dwindled and, aghast, she darted a glance at her son. 'You surely would *not* have… Constance is gently bred… She is a lady…'

'I am not guilty of seduction and abandonment,' William stated in a tone devoid of defensiveness. 'Constance might then have been young in years, but she was an experienced woman and knew her own mind. It was her decision to end our relationship.'

'You mean she was not… She had already…with *another*?' Pamela blurted, outraged.

William strode over to the window where he stared sightlessly out. 'I hope I am a gentleman, even when behaving as one is a trial. Consequently I have nothing more to add to what I have already told you. Other than perhaps if I had been more mature at the time, I would never have got involved with her at all.' As he turned back into the room, his eyes skimmed his father, digesting that Alexander's reaction to it all was to pinch his mouth whilst shaking his head.

'You and Constance seem friendly,' William addressed his mother. 'Has she ever hinted that her late husband was not the father of her daughter?'

William ignored his mother's amazement at such

plain speaking. His sympathy for her was scant; she had been mean to June throughout their marriage and his patience with acting tactfully in it all to keep a harmonious relationship with his parents, especially his father, was at an end. Blinkers had been lifted from his eyes and he saw himself as a coward, not a diplomat. At some time before the day was out he had to tell his beloved wife of a devastating possibility.

Had he not considered himself too dignified to bite at the tormenting bait Harley had been dangling, perhaps the rumour mill might not have ground on this long. The first whisperings from Harley and Darlington, making a mockery of his and June's domestic bliss, should have been nipped in the bud, in the time-honoured way of a man protecting the woman he loved. His passivity made his stomach churn with self-disgust and he flung his head back to combat the bile rising in his throat.

By the time his mother again had his attention her complexion was as grey-tinged as was his own. 'What is it? Have you remembered something?' William demanded.

'No, I have just thought of something. That shameless hussy might have foisted on you a bastard had you married her. How do you know she was not already increasing when you were betrothed?'

'It hardly matters now. I did not marry her, thank God!'

'To think *she* had the gall to reject *you*!'

Alexander seemed to surface from his brown study in a passionate mood. His perspiring face gleamed as ashen as his hair. Usually a man of impeccable etiquette, he exposed his uncontrollable anger in emitting an audible oath in the presence of his wife. It was followed by, 'I knew that woman was no good. She has never been any good. Why in damnation did she ever come up from Devon? All of the troubles started when she arrived in town.'

'I know,' William said bleakly. 'But I hope she would not attempt to drive June and me apart by resorting to spreading such spite.'

'Do you, indeed?' Alexander said quietly. 'I'm not convinced she is innocent in all this. She has ever had a sly look about her.'

As Pamela paced to and fro, alternately crushing her hanky in a hand, then stuffing it to her mouth, William stabbed a significant look at his father. Alexander nodded imperceptibly before saying to his agitated wife, 'There is nothing more to be done just now, my dear. Why do you not have a rest before dinner? You look to be overset.'

'Of course I'm overset!' Pamela shrieked. 'I have

no grandchild to call my own. All I have is a rumour that my son might have fathered a bastard—'

'There is no proof the child is mine!' William thundered across his mother's hysteria. 'If Constance is now out to cause mischief, she will find it will not work—'

'Oh, it is working very well,' Alexander interjected with great perception. 'I wonder, you know, whether Harley and that woman have cooked this up between them for some reason best known to themselves.'

As Pamela stifled a sob with her crushed scrap of lace, William said coolly, 'Heed good advice and take yourself off to rest, ma'am.'

Once Pamela was from the room Alexander gave his son a long look that mingled censure and sorrow. 'Have you told your wife any of this?'

William shook his head and a hand rose slowly to cover his face. 'No. And God knows I don't relish the prospect of doing so. But I must.'

'Indeed you must. It will reach her eventually…the poor mite,' Alexander said quietly.

William spun on his heel, shoved his hands deep into his pockets. 'My father-in-law knows, he thinks the attempt to blackmail me is of no consequence.'

'*Blackmail?*' Alexander exclaimed, throwing his hands up in despair.

William realised he had forgotten to mention that particular aspect of the disaster. He withdrew the note from his pocket. 'Edgar thinks this is the work of an opportunist. Possibly he is right.' He handed over the note for his father's perusal. 'First he thought that Constance Bingham might be the culprit.' A bleak laugh lodged in William's throat. 'She doesn't want for money. I imagine she could buy and sell the lot of us with what Charlie Bingham left her.'

Slowly Alexander raised his pewter head. His face was grimly set as he said ominously, 'Charlie Bingham was not the man he would have liked us all to believe in that respect either.'

Chapter Nine

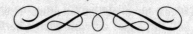

It was mid afternoon, not yet four of the clock when William entered his Mayfair townhouse. His demeanour was forbidding and all Herbert, his old retainer, received by way of greeting was a concise question.

If Herbert noticed that his response caused his master's tense countenance to relax, the butler was too professionally detached to betray his curiosity as to why Mrs Pemberton's absence was a relief. But as Mr Pemberton passed by, his rapid footsteps cracking against polished oak, his pace uninterrupted by their dialogue, Herbert's rheumy eyes followed the tall figure until it disappeared within a doorway. Then he shook his sparse-covered head.

Had William witnessed Herbert's sad gesture, his sombre mood would have darkened, for it surely indicated that not only was the *ton* whispering about his domestic problems, but his servants were too.

Once within his walnut-panelled study William prowled restlessly from desk to fire to window, all the while despising himself for a caitiff. June was still out on her afternoon drive with Gavin Blackmore, and he was thankful of the reprieve afforded him by another man paying attention to his wife. He gazed steadily through glass at swaying hornbeams, as though their graceful dance had entranced him. With a strangled oath he shoved away from the wide sash and in a moment had slumped into a leather wing chair positioned in a corner of the room. His head had barely appreciated the comfort of antique hide when, with a groan, he sprang up and was again tracing a triangular path across thick carpet.

A tumult of agonising thoughts was constantly battering his mind, but what gnawed at his sanity most was that shortly he must inflict on the woman he loved similar torment. He didn't want to be the one to cause her such anguish. Yet if he did not disclose today's distressing news, someone else most certainly would.

If he were too craven to admit to his youthful lechery, and its possible outcome, June's father would tell her simply to save her the humiliation of hearing it from the town tabbies. And William knew it was his place to protect June from such hurt. But by protecting her with that knowledge, he must also wound her deeply.

First he had to recall that particular incident and it was not something he could gladly do. He had banished the episode from his mind years ago. Had he exercised a little more self-control during his betrothal to Constance Palmer, he could have now dismissed this latest gossip as malicious fantasy. Instead he could not be sure that he was innocent of the latest accusation laid at his door.

There had been a single occasion when he and Constance had been intimate. His fiancée had hinted as soon as the betrothal contract was formalised that he need not wait for a plain wedding band to join the fancy gem he had given her before she act the wife for him.

It was no love match between them, but at the outset he had found Constance attractive in looks and character. He remembered feeling surprised and flattered that she should desire and trust him strongly enough to make such an offer. Virile and tender of years perhaps, but William had been brought up in his father's image. He had thus done the decent thing and an oblique refusal had been offered, couched in phrases containing honour and respect. Thereafter, when his chaste kisses were met with her teasing tongue and her body openly pliant against his, he began to reconsider his position. Her lowered eyes might have seemed demure, but her inquisitive fingers nudging close to his groin persuaded him she was insisting he accept the challenge.

So he did and soon fully understood why she had tempted him. It was not his desire she wished to slake, but her own. Beneath her pretty, girlish exterior was a woman of rapacious passion. It was no selfless demonstration of her loyalty or consideration that made her disrobe on a sultry August afternoon when they were, at her orchestration, alone, away from the other people enjoying a rout at her parents' mansion, and deep in lush Kent countryside. He was, at twenty, no novice in sensuality, having kept a mistress for several years, but no woman had ever played the whore for him with such tireless enthusiasm as Constance. He recalled he had felt at one and the same time fascinated and repulsed by the violence of her endless frustration. Time and again he had brought her to shrieking ecstasy, but it wouldn't do. Finally he had collapsed in long grass, exhausted and sated, and laughing in defeat. She had laughed too, scornfully, and tongued the vermilion welts on his chest, as though savouring that she had put them there, before determinedly straddling him again.

He understood many things after that, not least

why Sir Timothy and Lady Palmer seemed keen to quickly marry off their daughter, for doubtless her lusty appetite had previously threatened to disgrace them.

But William was a gentleman. The uneasiness over their future together had obsessed his mind during their quiet ride back to the Palmers' Kent mansion that sticky afternoon, yet he had not seriously considered betraying Constance by ending their betrothal. By the time he and his fiancée were again in company, William had resigned himself to several facts, one of which was that he had not taken his future wife's virginity. Miss Palmer was an insatiable wanton and he'd accepted that even his best efforts to hose the fire in her loins were likely to be unsuccessful. He'd expected to be, early in their marriage, a cuckold. Precociously cynical, he had reasoned that so were half the gentlemen of the *ton* who were, themselves, adulterers, regularly servicing another man's wife. He had decided it would be no real hardship to continue the *beau monde* tradition of marrying for convenience and forming a discreet attachment elsewhere.

Once his heirs were born, he would have allowed his wife her liaisons, so long as she was reciprocally discreet. Like his father before him, William decided to do the decent thing. The contract had been signed and sealed. He would have allowed himself to be led by the nose, straight down the aisle…and into a life of hell. For such it would have been, now he knew what a marriage could be.

Thankfully Constance and her parents had other ideas. They were not so troubled by conscience over a deal brokered with a young man of affluence but little influence. A nobler prospect had presented itself and William had been summarily dismissed. Lord Bingham had married Constance and made her a lady. But it transpired she had little else than her title to succour her in widowhood. Before he left his father's house this afternoon William had learned from Alexander that the city was now abuzz with some startling news.

It was widely known that Charles Bingham had speculated in overseas commerce prior to his death, but what had not been broadcast was that he had managed to conceal the spectacular extent of his portfolio's losses. Hoping to recoup some resources, he had then turned to an occupation destined to divest him of what little assets he retained. Charlie Bingham had privately wagered himself and his family into vast debt. The banks involved in loaning him money to shore up his foreign investments, and his reputation, were now impatient for repayment. Finally it had emerged that, far from leaving his wife rich, practically every piece of stock with which Constance Bingham was saddled was mortgaged to the hilt.

'Where are the best odds to be had, William?'

The soft melodic voice, the hint of teasing husking the words, dragged his blond head down in shame, for shortly he must dash that mellow mood. William stared at his white knuckles gripping at white marble as a rage of emotion threatened to sway him on his feet. The temptation to turn and crush his wife to him, beg her not to hate him, was not easily vanquished. But first there was much to be said...

Moments later, when June hugged him affectionately around the waist, William flinched. So deep had he been in his ravaging thoughts that he had not even heard the door open. He was unprepared and unequal to deal with the most daunting duty of his life.

June withdrew a little way from her husband's rigid back. She stepped a few paces to his right so she could study his profile. It was an unnecessary repositioning, for within a moment William had swung about and was gazing down into a pure sweet expression. June smiled, but as her husband's eyes jammed shut and an unsteady hand brushed his chin on its way to concealment in a pocket, her small teeth gripped her lower lip.

'What's the matter? Are you unwell?' June took in, with anxious hazel eyes, his pallor and the dark partings his agitated fingers had tunnelled through his fair hair.

'I will not gamble if you do not want. It was just that Mr Blackmore and I were talking of where we might get good odds and win some money. Horses or a boxing bout? Which to choose?'

'Gambling is for fools!' Her husband choked on a bitter laugh.

June eyed him with a dawning suspicion of the reason for this odd mood of his. 'You have not played at the tables this afternoon and lost heavily, have you?' It was a waspish nag, yet doubtfully uttered, for William had never been much of a gamester. 'Is that why you look so haunted? Are you feeling guilty?'

A bleak sardonic smile confirmed her correct. 'That is exactly how I do feel, June. God knows I'm feeling guilty.'

June felt an icy shiver at his raw irony, for it sounded so unlike her William's usual confident drawl. She put out her hands to hold him, but he caught at those two small comforts and held her rigidly at arm's length.

I'm feeling frightened, too, June, was a soulful whisper in his thoughts as his unwavering gaze drank in the sight of her beautiful topaz eyes and rich honey hair.

The ice stalking June's spine shivered tendrils to squeeze her heart. She had returned home determined to set her mind to helping Bethany Blackmore. Her first thought had been to find William and quiz him over sporting venues. Now, to her shame, Bethany's predicament was less important. How easy it was to lose charitable intentions when under threat oneself. With sinking heart, she instinctively knew who might be the menace. 'Is it new slanderous lies about you and that woman?' An increased pressure on her slender wrists curbed her movement to free herself. She allowed him to hold her, his thumbs grazing rhythmically over the translucent skin of her inner arms. After a deep breath, June said calmly, 'Well, you must tell me, William. If you do not, be assured someone else will.' When her husband seemed to struggle with inner decisions that aged his brow, she said on a sigh, 'Perhaps you were right. Perhaps we should have moved away from town. This constant anxiety over spiteful gossip is exhausting and stressful.'

William threw back his head, and sought solace from the ceiling, while attempting to conceal a spontaneous sheen in his eyes.

June observed it and, with a soft cry, launched herself against him. He allowed her hands, still imprisoned in his, to coil about his middle so she could cuddle him. 'Oh, William, what is it you must tell me this time?' she whispered against the muscular strength of his chest.

'I love you. I've always loved you. I have never in my life loved anyone else.'

The simple, hoarse declaration drew an enquiring little smile from his wife and she sought to gaze into his brilliant blue eyes.

'I want you to remember that. Whatever I tell you, that is the truth.'

June nodded and waited.

William suddenly withdrew from her embrace and walked away. By the window he turned, and seemed primed to speak. He hesitated, to put a hand against the sash. It had barely rested there a moment before it joined the other behind his back.

'The latest gossip is that I sired Constance Bingham's daughter.'

The declaration took barely a second to give out. There followed a hollow, seemingly interminable silence. Eventually, as though the gist of her husband's words had finally penetrated her mind, June fluttered a hand to her chest. It was a gesture of relief and a bubble of laughter erupted. 'Is that *all*?' A contemptuous cluck of the tongue was followed by, 'Harley and his cronies again, I suppose? How very silly these people are.'

'I am not sure whether Harley or someone else is to blame,' William said hoarsely. His voice was tinged with a betraying self-disgust that fired the first glimmer of suspicion to shock his wife's golden eyes wider. With a ragged indrawn breath William confessed, 'Much as I pray it is not so, I cannot dismiss it as impossible. The only way to know for sure if I justly stand accused is to go to Constance Bingham and demand the truth.'

June's complexion, already pale with strain, turned chalky. Slowly she moistened her lips then, as though in a trance, glided to the wing chair and put out a hand to clutch its back and steady her.

Watching her, a knife twisted in William's stomach and his hands clenched into fists. He wanted to rush to her to comfort her. Selfishly he also wanted her to succour him. Forgiveness, reassurance that she still loved him—he was prepared to beg on his knees for those things. But first there was yet more to say. He had not mentioned the blackmail note; as he remembered it two fingers pinched the paper in his pocket. He had thought Constance Bingham too wealthy to need such a paltry sum! With what he now knew of her financial circumstances he could draw no comfort there.

'It's a lie!' June whispered fiercely, splintering his feverish reflections. 'It's a ploy by that…that hussy. She has started this rumour because she knows you must then visit her and talk intimately before you can scotch it. She wants people to think it true. She intends you should abandon me and go to her. She is a scheming trollop!'

She got no further, for William strode across the carpet to take her into his arms and curb her hysteria. With a slap and a punch from two small fists clubbed together June freed herself. 'Don't you dare touch me!' she hissed. 'You say you have only loved me, yet you might have made a baby with Constance Bingham. You have made love to her.'

'I have not.' Realising how ridiculously inept that sounded, William added desperately, 'It was nothing like what we have together, June. It wasn't like that.'

'What was it like?' June shrilled.

William's fingers sank into his fair hair, momentarily clenched there as though he might rip some hanks of it out. 'It was…a long time ago. It's pointless talking of it, sweetheart,' he inadequately explained. His intention of calming his wife was thwarted by his inability to eloquently convey his regrets. His mind had been dulled with longing to have her back in his arms. June had so recently held him, looked at him lovingly. He wanted more. His arms stretched out, inviting…pleading with her to try a little conciliation.

June's response was to, with great deliberation,

lift the heavy tome on the table close by and hurl it, with good aim, straight at him.

Despite his anguish, excellent reflexes had William ducking out of danger and the book smashed into the mantel behind, knocking a Dresden falcon off its perch and into smithereens.

'No, you are right. It is pointless talking of it to *me*,' June concurred in a low quavering voice. 'You must go and talk to that woman and find out if she is indeed the mother of your bastard.' She tossed back the red-gold curls that were sticking to her wet cheeks. 'What will you do if she says it is so? Are we to be a *ménage à trois*?' June faced him with bitter challenge in her eyes. 'A *ménage à quatre*, I suppose it would be, if she brings the girl too.'

William strode to her and, gripping her by the shoulders, pulled her with a shake against him.

In a trice June had slapped and squirmed in his arms enough to make him let her free. 'I think I hate you. Yes, I do. I hate you very much.' Her shaky fingers wiped the moisture from her eyes.

'Listen to me!' William pleaded desperately. 'There is no proof I am guilty. What is indisputable is that someone intends us grave harm. The rumour could be concocted mischief. Many people know that Constance married Bingham with indecent haste after she jilted me.'

'After you were indecent with her, you mean?

Did you seduce her? How, I wonder, did Lord Bingham take that? How did that poor gentleman like discovering that you and his bride already had…had…' She stared violent-eyed at him. Part of her wanted to run and hide from the horror, yet another part desired to extract from him every sordid detail of his time with a woman who seemed to have the power to ruin her life. 'Was the child born soon after they married? Was it deemed to be a honeymoon baby?'

William nodded slowly. 'Yes. I recall that people congratulated them on soon starting their family,' he answered, with searing honesty.

A hand flew to cover June's mouth as though the escalating proof of what might be was nauseating.

Immediately William started towards her with such a determined step and look on his face that June fled to the door. 'I am going out,' she gasped. 'I have to go out,' she echoed in a whisper. 'I have made no arrangements yet for dinner. Perhaps you ought to dine at your club or ask cook to get you something.' Not once did she glance back before quitting the room.

'It will seem a little better in the morning.' Isabel was rocking her distraught younger sister in her arms, a hand stroking against June's silky berry-blonde hair. At an explicit look from his wife, the gentleman hovering uncertainly by the fireplace gratefully exited from the room. Shaking his head sadly to himself, Etienne sought the sanctuary of his study, where he sat pondering on how best he might help remedy the latest troubles afflicting the Meredith family.

June disengaged herself from Isabel's embrace. A pale hand went to smear the tears from her eyes. 'I feel as though my world is crumbling down about me.'

Isabel put an arm about her sister's shoulders and drew her close to drop a sympathetic kiss on June's brow. 'I know. It is a shock, but do not hate William too soon.'

'I do hate him!' June cried on a sniff.

'At the moment you think you do; but you must approve of his honesty. Would you rather he had tried to conceal this from you? Only think how you would have felt had you learned of the rumours when out and unprepared to deal with it.'

As that wisdom registered there was a softening in the tight line of June's mutinous mouth.

'William has not lied to you.' Isabel pressed home her advantage. 'He might have tried to deny any wrongdoing. In fact he is not yet judged guilty of any wrongdoing. He has acted decently, June, as he always does. The fact is, there is no proof that he has fathered the child.'

'But he has admitted that he and that woman were lovers! There is every likelihood it is true!' June choked. 'I am his wife and I yearn for his child, yet he might have made a baby with a woman who rejected him.'

'I know,' Isabel soothed. 'If it is true, it would be a very cruel twist of fate. But if it is not true, you are no worse off than you were yesterday. Your husband loves you and you love him.'

'I hate him!'

'You do not!' Isabel chided on a soft laugh. 'You are indignant because you have discovered he is human. It is as well you do not know all that Etienne got up to in his youth or you would brand him the veriest rogue.'

June looked at her sister through watery vision. 'Etienne is a good man. I like him very much.'

'I know. And I like William very much. And I would like it if you did not blame him for something he did before he even had met you.'

'He *is* to blame!' June raged, then closed her eyes for she knew how petulant she sounded. 'I am acting like a shrew,' she confessed on a wry laugh. 'I expect he will be glad to be rid of me.'

'I know he will be glad to have you home. William must be worried where you have got to.' Isabel took a glance at the clock in the corner as it chimed out ten.

June had arrived at their home in Eaton Square some two hours ago and had, at first, been too distraught to talk much at all about her troubles. Isabel had let her be until she had quietened, for she already knew what prompted her sister's distress. Earlier in the day Etienne had returned home to tell her worrying news of what he and Connor had overheard in White's. Beneath Isabel's charming air of serenity was simmering fury directed at the woman who seemed central to all June's woes. Isabel knew her sister, Rachel, was also of the opinion that it was high time Lady Bingham was on the receiving end of a tongue-lashing.

'I cannot go back there…not tonight,' June said, interrupting Isabel's thoughts. 'I cannot face William. I think I will not be able to act rationally in his company until some hours have passed. I suppose he must contact that woman. And if what she tells him is not good news…will I ever be rational again?'

'Indeed you will! No brass-faced baggage is about to ruin your happiness! And of course you must stay here tonight and very welcome too,' Isabel said briskly. 'I can soon find you some of my night things, then in the morning everything will seem better…you'll see…'

Chapter Ten

'Are you looking for Harley?'

The familiar male voice close behind barely penetrated William's consciousness as he strode into the hectic atmosphere of the Palm House gambling den. Certainly it did not slacken his unwisely rapid pace into a dim environment wreathed in aromatic fumes. William collided with a man holding a freshly replenished glass of whisky and, as the fellow muttered an obscenity, William returned him one more volubly.

Undeterred by this undeniable example of a foul mood, the gentleman pursuing William tugged at his arm to gain his attention. He succeeded in making his quarry swing about to reveal a gleam of bared white teeth. 'If you are looking for Harley, he is not here. He has gone to ground.' Adam Townsend was not rebuffed by his friend's snarl;

indeed, he gripped William's shoulder in a show of sympathy and support.

Aware that his arrival and this conversation were under surveillance, William indicated a more private spot by brusquely dipping his head at an empty alcove.

'I take it everyone knows why I'm here,' William said sardonically. A score or more pairs of eyes were now covertly observing their dialogue in that murky corner.

Adam nodded. 'Word has got round that you're likely to be riled enough to be out for blood. Harley is denying he had anything to do with this latest rumour. I have to say, much as I detest the weasel, I think he is telling the truth this time. He is not long returned from Brighton, and Darlington is yet there. The rumour mill started grinding when they were out of town.'

William gazed intently at his friend. 'I still want to talk to him. Do you know where he is?'

Adam grinned. 'I expect I might manage to find him…if that is what you want.'

'That is what I want.'

With a nod towards the door, Adam indicated he was ready to go.

'I've always wondered why you are such an inadequate, pathetic little man. Now I know.' With a frown of distaste and contempt curling his lip, William gathered the tumbled clothes from the threadbare chair and hurled them. 'For God's sake, put something on or I'll not know whether to laugh or commiserate. And it's certainly not for either of those reasons that I'm here.'

Harley snatched his breeches to his puny chest. Its grubby pallor looked as unhealthy as his facial complexion. He was infuriated by the disturbance, yet his black eyes slid nervously between the two men lounging inside his current paramour's tawdry boudoir. In his mind he was already beating an explanation out of the slut of a landlady who had allowed them to gain entry. No doubt the hag was so far in her cups she had forgotten her mistress already had a client. He slid a look at the comely doxy. She looked to be little older than nineteen, yet she was posing with professional ostentation behind a sheet clutched to her quivering white bosom.

As Adam Townsend glanced her way, Violet Smith lowered her eyes, and her linen.

Harley observed her at her tricks with sour interest. He was just a short while out of her bed and had received little satisfaction during the ten minutes he had spent in it. Already the little whore was soliciting for new company. 'How did you get in here?' Harley snapped sulkily, keen to soon get back to business and show Violet he was not a man to take short shrift.

'Same way you did,' William told him silkily. 'By crossing a palm with silver.'

Harley stomped behind a flimsy screen daubed with erotically entwined figures. Within a trice, peppered with expletives, he emerged, doing up his breeches. 'What do you want?'

'To talk to you.' William's tone was deceptively humouring.

'I've paid for sport, not conversation.' The bluster emerged from tight lips and with a slit-eyed threat for the languid woman on the bed he was soon sidling to the door in bare feet.

Benjamin Harley's bombast soon withered once they were out in the cold musty corridor of Number 12 Brick Lane, where Violet plied her trade along with a number of other enterprising young women with nothing to lose but their looks and desperation.

The hostile scrutiny of two pairs of hooded eyes soon had Harley unwisely scraping his soles on rough timber. 'I know why you are here and I had nothing to do with any of it.' It was a querulous announcement issued while he hopped away from splinters. His colour heightened as William's eyebrows rose quizzically.

Although they did not socialise in the same circles, Harley had thought he knew Pemberton. Here before him was not the placid chap he had care-lessly pilloried, safe in the knowledge that the man was too nice to retaliate.

For some while he and Colin Darlington had hap-pily fabricated tales about this man's renewed at-tachment to Lady Bingham without drawing reper-cussions. Too late he recognised, with awful clarity, that he had overstepped the mark and prodded a restful tiger to life. The William Pemberton con-fronting him was an unpredictable stranger and the way he was steadily watching him was making the hair on his neck eerily stir.

'It's true that Darlington and I made a joke and a wager about you and Constance Bingham be-ing…affectionate. But there was nothing malicious in it.' A whine of entreaty purred in Harley's nasal tone.

William's look of scepticism turned sardonic.

'And we wouldn't have taken it that far but for the lady making it plain she still pined after you. If Lady Bingham don't mind us being funny, why should you?' Harley shot an appealing look at Adam Townsend and received nothing but a stony stare in response.

'You thought what you did was funny?' William asked quite gently.

Harley managed to scuttle closer to Violet's door. Once he had the security of the handle turning within his grip, he recalled the pleasure awaiting him within. Emboldened by frustration, he jeered, 'I'm not frightened of you, Pemberton. You've never had the stomach for a fight. Have you brought along your friend to throw your punches for you?' He didn't want a response and had no intention of waiting for one. He was already sliding a leg through the aperture in readiness to dart neatly inside. A powerful hand spanning his throat, then leisurely closing on it, denied him his escape. Harley just had time to peer longingly at the crack of enticing yellow light before he was hauled away.

William, arm outstretched, his fingers an iron hasp on flabby flesh, took a casual pace closer to the man squirming against the wall opposite Violet's door. He lowered his head so his mouth was close to a side of Harley's blotchy, bloated complexion. 'I asked you a simple question that requires a simple answer. Do you think it funny to invent scandal about us and distress my wife?'

Harley just managed to shake his head, at which point William released his grip and the man caught a hoarse breath.

'Good,' William said brightly. 'I'll expect your full apology to us to be gazetted before the end of the week.'

Astonishment and fury mingled to make a comical study of the unlovely sight that was Benjamin's florid physiognomy. To submit to such a course of action would be unendurably humbling. He glowered at William whilst massaging life into his vocal chords. 'Apology?' he wheezed. 'You must have an attic to let if you seriously think I will—'

William turned back to inform the man with a traitorous amity, 'Be assured I think you will. Gazette an apology or ask Darlington to stand second for you and we'll settle this less lawfully. You may choose the secluded spot on which to expire and the manner of your despatch. In fact…let's do that. I'd like you and the rest of polite society to discover just how deadly serious I am.'

Benjamin Harley swiped his mouth with a hand that quivered. Never before had he, or anyone else, considered William Pemberton a man of action. Now he feared he could be a lethal adversary if he chose. 'I'll do it,' he muttered darkly and crept out of sight.

It was close to midnight when William wearily trudged into his chamber. His fingers loosened buttons as his eyes went immediately to the door that gave access to his wife's bedroom. A hand, unsteady at his mouth, betrayed his indecision whether to enter and recount where he had gone tonight in an attempt to start salvaging their marriage. He didn't want to waken her and see anguish return to haunt her tawny eyes. Worse still, he didn't want to see the hint of disgust that had made her retreat from him as though he was an adulterous monster.

Throughout their marriage he had been faithful and the idea that he might take a mistress was as alien to him as he knew it was to her. That he might contemplate divorce was laughable. June was all he had ever wanted; in her shyly sensual way she was far more erotic than Violet Smith or any such mercenary practitioners. As for Constance Bingham, her rampant sexuality might excite some men, but dogged fornication was not to his taste. June expected kindness and affection as a prelude to passion. She wanted to be wooed and he courted her now as tenderly as he had in their early honeymoon days.

Two hesitant paces were taken towards her room then, in a rush, he swept up the candle from the washstand and turned the handle.

A familiar floral scent wrapped about him like loving arms as he walked in the teardrop of golden light shed by the taper. Once close to the bed a draining sadness engulfed him as he gazed steadily at the undisturbed covers. The candle was deposited on her bedside table and, planting hands on hips, he bowed his head. An awful realisation swept over him that it was to be the first night of their marriage that he would sleep alone. The candle was snatched up, and so rapidly did he stride back the way he had come that the light was extinguished before he had fully retreated.

'You look in better spirits.'

June helped herself to toast and coffee from the sideboard and sat down at her sister's elegant dining table. 'You were right last night when you said I would feel better in the morning. I am now more rational.'

Isabel didn't look totally convinced by either her sister's smile or explanation. Nevertheless she nodded, and after a moment enquired, 'Have you been taking the herbal tincture I prepared for you?'

June wrinkled her nose as she complained, 'I have, and foul it tastes too! Yet despite you trying to poison me, I have persevered.'

Isabel sent her sister a significantly enquiring look.

June placed down her cup. 'Nothing to report, I am afraid, other than my menses last month arrived precisely on time, so that was a benefit of sorts, I suppose.'

''Tis often the case that the restorative must be taken for a while before a pregnancy results. But I know it can help. When I lived in York a local

woman conceived a daughter after ten years childless and three months of swallowing the brew.'

'It will take a little more than just the potion to
get me pregnant. I need a husband to help too.'

'And you have one.'

June's smile was brisk and courageous. She took
a bite of her toast. 'Are you going to the Sandersons' *musicale* tonight?'

Isabel nodded. 'And you and William must go
too.'

June tossed the toast crust to her plate at the mention of her husband's name. 'Yes, I know. We must
go and put on a brave face. I had already decided
that, if William is in agreement after the terrible
argument we had, we ought to act civil and pretend
nothing is amiss.' She sighed. 'William has ever
been a private man. He will not want it known the
troublemakers have succeeded in separating us.'

It sounded so easy now. The simple, sensible
statement betrayed none of the turmoil that had kept
her a sleepless guest in her sister's house while the
insufferably long hours ticked away and she longed
for the release of dawn light and a troublesome new
day.

'I don't think you are as right as you would have
me believe,' Isabel said softly, perceptively. 'I think
the June who arrived here in high dudgeon last
night was the right June.'

June drew her slender fingers through her autumn-gold hair. 'Oh, I still feel murderous,' she said with wry melancholy. 'But I am no longer sure who it is I must assassinate. And I accept that I still love William, although I would like to hate him…hurt him…as he has hurt me. And if it is proven that the child is his, I expect he will act honourably and not neglect his duty, although I would rather he ignore the hussy and her brat.'

'You would not have him act mean, June, and you know it.'

'No…I would not have him act mean. Not my Perfect William,' June said softly sour. 'The merry widow is wealthy, so I have the comfort that she will not be importuning at our door for money to keep a roof over her and her daughter's head.'

June noticed that comment prompted her sister to quickly chew her lower lip. 'I take it from your expression that even that small comfort is to be denied me. What have you heard?'

Isabel poured her coffee as she said gently, 'I'm sure it is not significant, but apparently Constance Bingham has no wealth. In fact, she has been saddled with her husband's debts. Far from coming to town with a fortune to lure a husband, it seems she is here to find herself a meal ticket.'

'So! It all becomes clearer. William will be distraught to know it is not him but his cash that is attractive,' June sniped caustically. She rose in a swish of skirts from the table and stepped to the window. 'I am not going to say another word on the matter, for what will be will be,' she announced quietly. 'William must do what he thinks best to sort it out, and I am going to do what I had planned to do yesterday, before I learned I had married a stranger. A certain cure for one's own woes is to reflect on a worse misfortune endured by others.'

Isabel's expression made it clear she required an explanation for such philosophy. June obliged with, 'Gavin Blackmore and I have become good companions. He was telling me just yesterday how terribly his younger sister has suffered. Neither he nor Bethany had a very happy childhood in the parsonage where they grew up. Now his sister's plight is so much worse. Yesterday I was determined to help her, for the poor woman is incarcerated in the Fleet prison.'

Isabel's green eyes widened with shock. 'Gavin Blackmore? He is an old school friend of William's, is he not?'

June nodded. 'He gained a scholarship and excelled academically, although he seems a little defensive about his origins as a clergyman's son.' She sighed impatiently. 'How bad of me! I promised Gavin I would not repeat what he told me about Bethany's plight to anyone at all.'

'Your secret is safe with me, June,' Isabel said a trifle indignantly. 'I would not break your trust.'

At June's small grimace of acceptance, Isabel continued, 'How on earth did a gently bred lady get into such a pickle?'

After just a brief hesitation at disclosing more, June concisely recounted Bethany Blackmore's history.

Having listened to the woman's hellish ordeal, Isabel simply raised her eyebrows in disbelief. 'And her brother does not have the wherewithal to purchase her freedom?'

June shook her head. 'Gavin has told me little about his circumstances and I have not liked to pry, for I fear it might embarrass him to admit he has not done as well as his peers. He seems a proud man but, despite his fine education, it seems Gavin has not prospered as well as he ought. I believe he has made a career brokering insurance, for he mentioned attending to such a business in Devon. I'm sure William would loan him the money needed to free Bethany, but Gavin will not hear of it. He became quite sharp with me when I hinted at such. As I said, he seems independent and will not accept charity under any circumstances. But I gave him some clothing to take to his sister, for Bethany has had her possessions stolen by rowdy women in gaol.'

Isabel shook her head, sending her pretty curls rippling about her shoulders. 'For a lady to endure such treatment…oh, it doesn't bear thinking about.'

'Tonight at the Sandersons' *musicale*, I shall keep myself occupied at the card table,' June announced. ''Twill give me something to do and if I am lucky enough to win some money, I shall put it aside for Bethany Blackmore.'

'You are back then.'

'Of course,' June responded in an equally cool tone as that used by her husband. 'Did you expect I might have run away from home?' This was added with a slanting flash of topaz eyes as she stripped off her gloves, then whirled about to fully face him.

'Where did you stay last night?' William curtly interrogated.

'I stayed with my sister Isabel.' June found it easier to keep her tone light as his grew harder.

'And you didn't think to send word to let me know where you had gone or that you would be out all night?'

'There are many times when you are abroad and I have no idea where you have gone. I have not before thought it necessary to check on your whereabouts. Perhaps I have been regretfully naïve.'

'Only once have I stayed out all night and you

knew I was with Etienne at my club. So what in damnation is that supposed to mean?'

'It means that if I were more sophisticated, I might cope better with knowing I have married a libertine…'

His hand slammed against a wall, abbreviating June's further censure. William closed his eyes and two fingers momentarily pinched at strain between them. 'Am I to be condemned as an insufferable rake because I once was intimate with a woman to whom I was engaged?'

June felt a tightening in her throat at the mention of the horrible fact. A part of her mind recognised she was being unfair, but it was impossible to control the pain of knowing that she was childless yet her husband might already be a father. 'You might have made Constance Bingham pregnant…' Her voice was raw with accusation.

'I know…'

His voice was husky with apology, but its soothing tenor only stoked her angry frustration and she hissed, 'My husband has a daughter with his former fiancée and I am supposed to just *accept* that?'

'June…' William sighed in the exasperated tone of a man unsure whether to be authoritative or supplicating. He walked closer to her and pulled her against him, curbing her resistance with strong arms. 'I don't want it to be true. I'm sure it is not true,' he crooned gruffly through the lump in his throat. His hands cradled her head, tightened in emphasis. 'I love you.'

June pushed at his shoulders, looking into his distraught face through blurry vision. 'You have not yet been to see Constance Bingham?'

'No. I wanted first to speak to Benjamin Harley to find out if he has fabricated more gossip.' He sighed his disappointment. 'Unfortunately I think he is telling the truth when he says this latest rumour is not his doing. He admits to spreading those other lies about a mistress and a divorce and is to gazette an apology to us.' As June's eyes widened in surprise a hand gently cupped her cheek. 'Oh, he is not genuinely sorry. He would be pleased to know his scheming has had such a profound effect on us.'

June's soft mouth hardened. 'One thing I did decide upon last night was that I would hate to give our tormentors the opportunity to gloat over how they have broken us.'

'I feel just that way. There, we still suit,' he said with wry humour in his tone. When a side of her tight lips involuntarily tugged into a small smile he dipped his head to steal a quick kiss, pursuing her and defeating her evasion.

Uncaring of the fact that they were in full view should any of the servants wander into the vestibule, William slipped his hands inside his wife's coat and moved her closer to him. When he kissed her this time it was no gentle salute. His mouth captured hers, moulded to hers with a fiery urgency that made June's blood throb at her temples.

'I missed you so much last night!'

'Yet you didn't think to come and find me?' June returned archly, her lips still pulsing from the heat of his kiss.

'I did come and find you. I knew you stayed at Isabel's for our carriage was stationed outside their door. Did you want me to come in and get you? I nearly did.'

Isabel quickly looked up into her husband's sultry low-lidded gaze. 'You knew I stayed there?'

'As soon as I realised you were not at home I scoured the streets of every conceivable place I thought you might be. I went to your parents' address first, of course... Oh, they didn't know,' he reassured on seeing her immediate anxious look. 'I stayed outside and would only have let it be known you were missing had I not managed to locate you somewhere. I have not had a wink of sleep all night,' he complained.

'Neither have I!' June retorted with asperity.

'We are both tired then and ready for bed.'

William's sultry suggestive tone made his wife blush and just for a moment laugh. Oh, how skilfully could her husband manoeuvre her into submission!

'Come,' William invited huskily. 'Let's go upstairs…'

'No,' June said quietly but in a voice that quavered with resolve. 'Can't you see it won't do? No!' She turned her head as he made to kiss her again. 'It solves nothing, William…' Her tone was raw with despair.

'It does for me,' William said bluntly before he turned and left her.

Chapter Eleven

'I am not surprised he is grown bored with her.'

'Neither am I. That gown she has on is as prim as the one my mother is decked in. She dresses so matronly, yet has no babe-in-arms as an excuse for it. What did an attractive man like him ever see in her?'

'I have always thought he could have done better for himself. His mother makes it plain that she thinks so too.'

'He once wanted to marry a woman who does herself up in scraps of muslin.'

'Wanted to? He did marry her…in all but name. If the gossip I've heard is true, perhaps she has their daughter to prove it.'

The disembodied dialogue was replaced by the sound of two women tittering. Their shrill amusement finally broke the spell that held June shocked and unmoving at the entrance to the ladies' with-drawing room. She took a hasty step back from the threshold, remaining unseen.

June and Isabel had moments ago been on the point of entering this sanctuary set aside by the San-dersons so their female guests could rest and refresh themselves. Isabel had diverted to speak to an old friend and as June loitered, lost in her own thoughts, waiting for her sister to return, she had paid little attention to the snippets of conversation that had drifted to her ears. Over some minutes she had assimilated the significance of what was being said. She had tensed, straining to listen through in-furiatingly deafening blood pounding in her skull. Even had she not heard William's name being men-tioned, other clues would have indicated that she was the object of scorn.

She recognised her detractors from their voices. Julia Lake and Monica Dawson were spinsters in their early thirties. Neither had managed to lure a husband in their prime and now they were united in feeling particularly sour towards well-married ladies.

June would have liked to burst in and tell those spiteful spinsters a few bald truths, but she hesi-tated. Not so very long ago she might have re-mained nonchalant on overhearing her appearance judged and her husband pitied for his choice of wife. With the rift between William and her widening inexorably, she felt vulnerable to doubts and picked over what the vinegary misses had said, wondering if perhaps there was truth in their criticism.

A quick glance down at her turquoise silk gown confirmed it was modest in style, yet this evening when she had descended the stairs, William had steadily watched her from his vantage point, propped against a doorframe. Acutely aware of his low-lidded appreciation she had felt almost triumphantly alluring. There might be friction between them, they might be conversing shortly, but William could not conceal his admiration. In his eyes she was beautiful.

June proudly raised her chin and, seeing that Isabel was still engaged with her friend, gathered up those dowdy skirts in tight fists, summoned up a smile, and went to join the company.

'I say, steady on, Pemberton. That's the third glass of champagne you've downed in half an hour. If you carry on like that there'll be none left for the rest of us. I thought you steady chaps favoured small beer.' The jovial gentleman who had spoken grimaced disappointment at the cards he'd been dealt and discarded his hand.

'I recall a time when he had a partiality for warm

lemonade. He was a stalwart at Almack's every Wednesday when he was courting. My nieces regularly graced that noble marriage mart while poor old Edgar regularly moped about the pillars like a wallflower, looking miserable as sin.' Edgar's brother-in-law, Nathaniel Chamberlain, had introduced that humorous anecdote about the *ton*'s premier matchmaking assembly before lounging back comfortably in his chair and winking with pleasure at the monarchs fanned in a hand.

'So would you have looked miserable,' Edgar moaned to the happy gamester, 'with the prospect of all those débuts paring down your bank balance. Not to mention the prospect of all those nervous chaps pacing back and forth in your drawing room, wearing out your carpet.' He shook his head to himself. 'It's not to be recommended. Oh, no. Not to be recommended by me at all.' He glanced fondly at William. 'Of course, we were more than happy with the outcome for our girls. Fine husbands so far…every one of them,' he added with emphasis.

William sipped at his champagne and inclined his head in acknowledgement of Edgar's compliment. 'From a nervous chap's point of view, it's a relief when his courting days are over. Luckily I won't again need to enter Almack's.'

'Don't be too sure of that,' Edgar warned his son-in-law. 'You might yet have a brace or more of daughters to settle, and be again fed bread and butter and warm lemonade, while you observe the sweet chits fluttering about in their finery. Take my word on it, with every single one of 'em, you won't know whether to encourage the scoundrel who's caught her eye or to call him out.' He shuddered at the reminiscence. 'In truth, I didn't like losing them, you know.'

'You've still got Sylvie to keep you company in your dotage,' William ruefully reminded him.

Edgar smiled. 'Yes…my Sylvie can stay home and keep her old papa happy. She's not in a rush to grow up. Sensible girl.'

'I'll put down a wager that in ten years' time we see Pemberton's chit in the marriage mart. Why, she will be all of eighteen by then.'

In the wake of that smirking aside settled an uneasy silence. Colin Darlington sauntered closer to the table. Benjamin Harley, another new arrival at the Sandersons' *musicale*, hurried closer, glaring an explicit warning for he had sensed a dangerous atmosphere fomenting. Darlington was only recently returned to town and Harley had not had an opportunity to bring him up to date with what had transpired in his absence.

'Ah, Darlington, back from Brighton, I see,' William drawled. 'Sea air quite chill, was it? Come and join us. Sit down and warm up your brain.'

The speaking stare Benjamin Harley was directing at his crony became pronounced enough to crane his neck. Finally he resorted to beckoning frantically. Darlington stabbed a poisonous look William's way, but allowed his friend to steer him away without countering the insult. The retreating men were so engaged in their hissing conversation that they didn't notice the woman they passed or the dismay they had caused her.

June had been on the point of joining William and her father at the table in the hope of winning a tidy sum to hand over to Gavin Blackmore for his sister. Twice this evening her progress had been halted on overhearing hurtful gossip about her or William.

She watched her father glaring at Harley and Darlington before he reached over and grasped William's arm in a show of support. As June's misty eyes focussed, she realised William was looking at her. After a heady heartbeat in which she felt engulfed by the strength of his regret and sorrow at what she had witnessed, he smiled. His whole demeanour exuded a plea that she would not allow this paltry incident to worsen things between them.

'Are you ready to join the gamblers?'

June pivoted about to see Adam Townsend just behind her, mischievous laughter in his eyes.

He took her hand and placed it on his arm. 'Let's

see if we can relieve these gentlemen of a few sovereigns.'

Having taken a deep, inspiring breath, June rose to the challenge. 'Yes, let us do just that. I have a good cause for a few spare sovereigns.'

'Ah, let me guess,' Adam said with a twinkling smile. 'You have seen an indispensable something in the modiste's that's newly opened in Starling Street.'

About to shyly chide him for his chauvinistic levity and declare she had a less selfish use for her winnings, June changed her mind and simply laughed. 'How *did* you guess?' She had promised not to repeat what Gavin Blackmore had told her of his family's misfortunes and, although she implicitly trusted her sister Isabel, she felt a little guilty at having revealed even to her Bethany's plight.

Adam chivalrously ejected the nearest fellow from his seat at the crowded table to offer it to June. The young buck goodnaturedly waved away June's apology with a stuttered, 'My…my pockets aren't dee-deep enough anyhow…'

Once settled, June bestowed on her father a fond smile before acknowledging the other gentlemen with a gracious dip of her burnished blonde head. Then she looked at her husband. But the appeal and apology that she had seen in his eyes moments ago, which had wrenched at her heart, were gone.

With a woman's intuition June knew he was still smarting from her rejection earlier that day. With a wife's intuition, she also knew that she was right to want a more permanent solution to their problems than an hour or so of amorous abandonment…even if it was delightful. The memory of a mere kiss from him made an involuntary little *frisson* tingle along her skin. His artful hands could move and smooth away her anger and hurt and insist she forget everything but what pleasure would come next…

With a quick lift of her head she gave William a scintillating smile; it caused him to quirk an indolent eyebrow at her.

William was not fooled by her *faux* gaiety, but eventually his sardonic expression mellowed and a reciprocal slow smile tugged at his lips. His wife blushed prettily beneath his sultry regard, but her eyes defied him beneath a web of lashes. It couldn't have been plainer had she clearly said, 'The answer is still no.' William's fingers tightened on the cards he held before he dropped them to the baize. As a small growl of mirthless laughter gazed his throat, his father-in-law, seated next to him, sent him a quizzical look.

William observed that the gentlemen about the

table were exchanging knowing glances. He could guess what they were thinking and the irony was not lost on him. *They appear fond even if it is gossiped he has a love child in Devon.* The words seemed to hover unspoken in the atmosphere and, looking at June's contained composure, he sensed she knew it too. William felt irritated enough at the sham to want to shove back his chair and walk away. But his wife was where he wanted her, close to him, and they were united in wanting to appear harmonious. Why fret that the subterfuge was working? 'Shall I deal?' he suggested.

'What are we playing, gentlemen?' June asked. 'Faro? *Vingt-et-un*? Oh, some cash, please, William…' she sweetly tacked on to the end while airily extending a slender white hand towards him.

Adam Townsend, who had stationed himself behind June's chair, leaned over a demurely bared white shoulder. A pile of coins was deposited on the table. 'Allow me…I insist, for I know the lady has in mind a good cause for any winnings,' he amiably explained to June's flint-eyed husband.

'You were lucky tonight.'

'Yes…wasn't I…' June replied and chinked the coins held inside her glove. She continued gazing at the night scene as the carriage moved along although she could feel the strength of her husband's stare singeing the side of her face.

'I didn't mean your winnings,' William advised with mild irony. His eyes drifted over June's moon-lit profile. 'What I mean, my love, was that had you and Townsend flirted just a moment or two longer I might have had to intervene. Blackmore has a serious rival, it seems.'

June tilted her head, stripped off a glove and let warm coins drop, one by one, on to her palm. 'I never flirt, William, you know that. I was married before I learned that art. And Gavin Blackmore is your friend and amiable and courteous to me, nothing more. You surely aren't jealous? Whatever for? I'm the sensible Meredith girl…modest and demure, everyone knows that.'

'Of course I'm not jealous. I'm a dull, peaceable chap. Everyone knows that, too. But I could change.'

June's eyes flicked to her husband, for the tone he had used chilled her. Their shining eyes tangled in the gloom. She cocked her head and countered slowly, 'Yes…I could change, too…'

Gavin Blackmore looked at the small curled fingers close to his chest, then up at a sweet expression. 'I take it from your happy countenance that I'm not in danger of a punch from that fist.'

'Guess what I have for you…or rather for Bethany.'

Gavin shook his head. 'I don't think it is a pair of woollen stockings concealed in there.'

Laughing, June took one of his hands and dropped with a chink and a glint four half-sovereigns on to his palm.

Gavin looked at her with amazement then bowed his head. He made to return the coins, but June quickly foiled his reluctance to accept the money by curling his large fingers over the gold. 'I was lucky last night. Adam Townsend and I were partners at cards. Had he not partnered me I expect I might now be offering you a farthing, for I have always before been bad at playing. Adam is a fine player.'

Gavin twisted a smile. 'As I said before, Townsend is blessed in lots of ways.' Almost thoughtlessly the sovereigns were slipped into a pocket while he chuckled. 'How satisfying that the money has been donated in a roundabout way by the high and mighty Earl of Malvern.'

June frowned at him. 'I think Adam seems… nice…not at all high-handed.' The praise was muted, but made Gavin shoot a measuring look at her.

'As I said before, Townsend has a winning way with the ladies, too.' Gavin shrugged his indifference. Gathering up the reins, he shook them over the sleek and supple backs of William's matched greys. 'This is a fine equipage. Do you drive it? Does William allow it? I know more and more ladies are driving their own carriages. Some of you young women are quite daring in your sporting exploits.'

'I've never been of a daring disposition.' June grimaced a laugh. 'But I had a try at taking the ribbons once on a piece of common land. I can't say I was very successful. In fact, but for William's help I might have turned the thing over. William said I ought to try again.'

Gavin looked mock-horrified. 'Did he indeed? Your husband is a brave man. I would have imagined he might have banned you from trying a second time in case you came to some harm.'

'William can be surprisingly liberal. He is not at all as sober and predictable as people think.'

Gavin was quiet for a few moments, then mentioned, 'I think you are an uncommonly understanding wife to deal so well with the recent scurrilous gossip concerning your husband. William is a fortunate man to have your loyalty, no matter there is no truth in any of it.'

June's lips twisted wryly. 'We do our best to carry on regardless, but it has not been easy. I cannot honestly claim not to have been shocked and upset by it all but… Oh, enough of it! Come, you earlier promised to tell me how Bethany is doing. I should like to visit. I am not daunted by the thought of entering the Fleet to see her. Will that money I have given you help bring her closer to being released?'

'Her debts are heavy.' Gavin's answer was shortly given. 'And I would not dream of letting you set one foot inside that hell-hole. Your husband would kill me should he ever find out I had taken you there.' A hand was put up to silence June's protest. He continued with a sad shake of the head, 'Her gaolers demand bigger bribes. But I must keep her properly fed or she will succumb to disease. Dysentery and consumption are constant threats.'

Gavin turned to look at her with a sheen enhancing the brown of his eyes. 'Bethany asked after you. When I took her those things you had donated she wept. She sends all her best wishes to you and her grateful thanks.'

'And I send her back equal good wishes. I know those coins won't release her…but if they buy her some meagre privileges and her health, it is something.'

Gavin nodded. 'What you have donated so far has been a great help and so very well received. Once the turnkeys have their bribes she feels a little safer. She need not huddle the day and night away in a corner trying to stay inconspicuous.'

'Does she need their protection? Is she frightened still of the other women? Do they still steal her things?'

'The women she is incarcerated with are of the vilest nature, but the gaolers are a worse menace. Bethany is a pretty girl. It is not a place for a genteel lady to be. Those lecherous swine have no respect for virtue or good breeding.'

As June understood his meaning colour flooded her cheeks. 'We must get Bethany free as soon as we can,' she said earnestly.

Gavin urged the horses to a faster pace. 'Indeed we must…' he murmured.

Gloria Meredith poured her son-in-law's tea with a hand that shook. The emotion causing her ague was anger, not a nervous disposition. Etiquette decreed it would be unseemly for her to take William to task over yet more gossip that had come to her ears. But, if there was truth in it, she had no intention of letting William escape without he took with him a flea in his ear. With that in mind she was hoping to keep him here until her husband returned and decided whether he deserved to be hauled over the coals. With a forcefulness that slopped liquid into the saucer, William's cup was banged down on the table at his side.

William glanced enquiringly at his mother-in-law, for he had sensed in her an unusual hostility as soon as he entered her house this afternoon.

His reason for visiting was a hope that he might come upon June here. His wife was rarely to be found at home during the day. His friends were allowed to escort her on shopping trips or drives in the park whereas his efforts to take her out were coolly rebuffed. Her sisters and parents were regularly treated to her company, yet she stayed out of his. He now knew June was being squired about town this afternoon by Gavin Blackmore. He had prised that much information from his mother-in-law's pursed lips before, with seeming reluctant duty, she insisted he have some refreshment and swept away.

William took a sip from his cup and took stock. Momentarily his eyes closed. He was out of favour everywhere it seemed. Even Adam Townsend had had a prior appointment with his mother and had tarried but a little while to talk in Boodle's.

Only one individual had made it clear they would welcome his company today and it was someone he wished to avoid seeing at all costs. The infernal woman causing problems in his life had responded coyly to the note he sent her demanding an unequivocal answer to a single question contained therein. A simple yes or no would suffice, he had suggested in his second letter, when the first had prompted Constance Bingham to return him a missive spanning two lengths of parchment that revealed nothing other than her desire that they meet privately to talk.

William glanced at Gloria's stern profile, wondering whether her aloof attitude was due to the fact that she had already got wind of his visit to Lady Bingham's residence in Park Lane. In view of the fact that he had come here straight from there, it seemed unlikely she would know of it, but then the speed at which gossip travelled no longer amazed him.

The fact that his erstwhile fiancée would not confirm or deny the rumours until he danced to her tune and visited her had vastly exasperated William. He knew that June would hate to discover he had paid Constance a visit. Yet equally he knew that their wounds would never heal until it was discovered whether he had sired Constance's daughter. On receipt of Lady Bingham's response that morning he had at a respectable hour in the afternoon gone, unannounced, straight to see her, only to find her already abroad. Oddly he had felt vexed rather than relieved that she was out. Having taken his courage in both hands and forced the dreaded visit upon himself, he was immensely peeved to find the effort squandered.

'I wish Edgar were here to speak to you,' Gloria suddenly burst out, shattering William's moody introspection. 'But as he is not, there is something *I* must say…for enough is enough…'

William was frowning in bemusement at his mother-in-law when a servant entered and announced that Lord Malvern was waiting in the hall and wished an audience.

Gloria looked surprised, but instructed the servant to show him in.

In the event it was Edgar Meredith who ushered Adam Townsend into the cosy room, having returned home just minutes after his visitor arrived. 'How opportune, both of you are here together. Just the two *gentlemen* I wanted to see,' Edgar snarled in greeting.

Chapter Twelve

'Have you now a taste for scandal?'

Having bellowed out his opening salvo, Edgar cast a frown at the door. His wife had excused herself so he was not anxious for her delicacy. Besides, Gloria was aware of the nature of William's alleged crime. What worried Edgar was that his raised voice might bring the servants to queue at the keyhole. In a low hiss he continued, 'I have to say that I am now heartily sick of having my family—my daughter June in particular—made the butt of gossip because of the way you have conducted yourself. William Pemberton, the quiet man, the steady fellow…hah!'

'What is that supposed to mean? What in damnation is going on now?'

William's tone was weary, but the speed with which he lithely unwound from his chair alerted

Edgar to the fact that his son-in-law's temper was
as volatile as his own.

Without waiting for his father-in-law's reply,
William enquired sharply of his friend, 'Are you
here to meet my wife?'

'Not specifically, but I believe she might soon
arrive.'

'What makes you think so? Have you seen her?
I believed her to be shopping with Blackmore this
afternoon.' William knew he must sound tediously
possessive, but June's preference for any company
other than his was deeply irritating him, and he no
longer felt inclined to feign nonchalance over it all.
Yet how could he blame her for withdrawing from
him? She was the innocent in it all. She did not
deserve to have her contentment stripped away.
They could have coped with the gossips and Harley's malice. It was the regrettable liaison in his
youth that was the stumbling block to regaining
happiness. And he shouldn't seek to deprive June
of her gallants. At least if she was out socialising
it might keep her spirits up and her worries at bay.
The fault was his. The blame was his alone. He
sighed.

Adam gave his beleaguered friend a disarming
smile. 'There is no intrigue, I promise. A few hours
ago I was escorting my mother about the shops in
Regent Street when we ran into your wife and

Blackmore. My mother invited Mrs Pemberton and her sisters to an impromptu gathering she arranged this morning for five o'clock this afternoon. I believe there are to be other débutantes present with their mamas and your wife thought it would be an excellent opportunity for her youngest sister to socialise. I expect they will all be attending the same balls and assemblies. As time is short I am here to convey the invitation to Mrs Meredith. Your wife has gone to speak to her married sisters about the invitation.' Adam hesitated, looked quizzically at his friend. 'Do you mind?' The query was laden with mockery. 'I assure you they will like it. My mother is a capable hostess.'

A capable hostess? Lady Rockingham was known to be one of the *ton*'s most popular and influential ladies. If Sylvie were to be taken under her wing, the success of her début would be assured. William muttered on a sigh, 'Of course I have no objection to your mother's invitation.' A hand illustrated his apology.

'Well, this is all very nice!' Edgar huffed. 'The two of you discussing respectable ladies' tea parties when I have the task of speaking of women of a very different class.'

Edgar drew himself up, his head waggled on his neck as a haughty glance whipped between the two cultured gentlemen. 'Lord Malvern is single and thankfully his conduct is of no consequence to me or to my family. You, sir, are married to my daughter and your morals and behaviour have an impact on us all.'

'God's teeth!' William snapped impatiently. 'Am I to ever be advised why I stand accused this time?'

'Indeed you are!' Edgar retorted. He inclined closer. 'And quickly, before June arrives, for I do not want this tawdry tale to reach that innocent's ears. She has been hurt and humiliated enough.'

William strode in exasperation to the window while he waited to be advised of his crime. 'Gentlemen, you were both spotted in a place frequented by low life. If you must go there, sirrah,' his son-in-law received a narrow-eyed glare, 'perhaps you ought to be more discreet.'

William, whose thoughts were cluttered with many things, still looked baffled, for he detected few clues in the homily to jog his memory.

'It would not be quite so bad if you had not been spotted entering together the strumpet's bedchamber. One at a time would have been preferable, for better to be thought lechers than deviants.'

William and Adam simultaneously made sense of Edgar's lecture. Adam's expression showed he was undecided whether to laugh or protest. His friend's latent amusement simply darkened William's scowl.

'And don't think to deny it.' Edgar dismissed anticipated excuses with an airy gesture. 'I have the information first-hand from a reliable source. Unfortunately, my wife was, unbeknown to me, in the vicinity when the gentleman spilled the beans, so she knows too.' Edgar shook his head. 'Gloria is again agitated. She is gravely worried for June's health and happiness. How much more can that poor mite take?'

'There is nothing at all about that incident that need disturb my wife.'

'You might think so, but women don't see it that way,' Edgar philosophised, having taken a sophisticated view of his son-in-law's remark.

William gave Edgar an exasperated look, but decided against further explanation or defence.

'I have a curiosity to know the identity of your friend who frequents a Brick Lane whorehouse,' Adam mentioned while studying his nails.

Something in the way his lordship speared a stare at him from beneath his dark brows made Edgar redden and bluster, 'Well, I hope you don't think it was me! A hovel like that!' A hand dusted his coat sleeve as though a mere thought of the place might contaminate him.

'It doesn't matter who it was,' William interjected impatiently. 'My reason for being there had nothing to do with any doxy or the services on offer. We went there—unwisely, now I think on it for God knows everything I do seems to be under surveillance—to find Harley. With hindsight I admit it was rash to go to a bawdy house, but at the time I was irate and set on extracting an immediate promise from that weasel that he would make a public apology to us. He has kept to his word. *The Times* carries the piece today if you care to check on it.'

'Are you stalked wherever you go? I feel guilty for having revealed where Harley was. I can vouch for his innocence,' Adam told Edgar.

'Harley? Does *he* go there too?' Edgar sounded shocked. 'I imagine Nathaniel doesn't know *that*!' he muttered to himself.

'Nathaniel Chamberlain?'

Edgar turned florid on realising he had inadvertently betrayed his informant as being his sister's husband. He had always got on famously with Nathaniel, which was more than could be said for his overbearing sister. 'Well, we are all men of the world. My sister's health is not good and Nathaniel is a considerate chap...' He mumbled that out in his brother-in-law's defence before he strode two paces back and forth. 'The point is that, with the gossips out for blood, it was not wise to have been seen in such a place. Popular she may be, but it is not as though Violet Smith could boast a certain...*distinction*...' he chose the word carefully before adding on a sly nod '…as can those demi-reps who like to keep company with this fine fellow.'

Adam Townsend remained impassive in the face of that compliment.

'I am conscious of the difference,' William said in an exceedingly dry tone.

'What is a demi-rep, Papa?' Sylvie Meredith had slipped inconspicuously into the room.

Edgar visibly winced at the untimely intrusion by his youngest daughter. He cleared his throat and mumbled in embarrassment, 'Umm, well, never you mind. You should not barge in, but knock first, you know, young lady. Did you not hear me talking to these gentlemen?'

Sylvie flushed slightly at the rebuke, but her chin lifted and her violet eyes searched a sternly handsome face as though she might detect an answer there.

'Sylvie!' Edgar chided as his daughter remained where she was and continued to gaze boldly at his aristocratic visitor. 'Now come along, my dear, go from here! I was having a private talk with your brother-in-law and his lordship. They will think your manners sadly lacking.'

'Why? All the time I am told I must improve and grow up, yet when I ask a question I get no answer. How will I learn things?'

'The expression refers to a lady of doubtful character,' Adam quietly satisfied her curiosity.

'Thank you, sir.' Sylvie smiled at Adam. 'You see, I am not about to swoon on knowing it, Papa.'

'Sylvie!' Edgar sped to his daughter's side and, snatching her arm, firmly steered her to the door. 'You will have Lord Malvern think you the silliest girl—'

'*Au contraire*…I don't think that at all. Besides, it is on Miss Sylvie's account that I am here.'

Sylvie swirled about, freeing her arm from the parental grip. 'You are here to see me?'

'Yes,' Adam said in voice that had become husky.

'Are you going to take me for a ride at last?'

Aware that her father and her brother-in-law were watching him curiously, Adam added crisply, 'I ought speak to your mother. Naturally you are both invited out. Would you find her for me?'

Sylvie nodded her brilliant blonde head and in a moment was gone.

'This is most unexpected…but very welcome, sir.'

Adam smiled politely on learning that Mrs Meredith gladly accepted his mother's invitation. His eyes involuntarily veered towards the woman's daughter. The angelic chit seemed only interested in teasing her papa over his failure to beat her at chess the previous evening.

Gloria had also noticed Sylvie's indifference to this precious opportunity. In common with William, Gloria recognised that Lady Rockingham's patronage, once gained, would be of invaluable help in making Sylvie's come-out a triumph. She could think of several acquaintances, with daughters to be launched this season, who would give their eye-teeth for such influential backing.

Suddenly aware that Lord Malvern looked ready to depart, Gloria quickly said, 'Oh, my apologies! How remiss of me. You must take tea, sir.' Feigning deafness to Adam's excuse that, on the contrary, he must take his leave, Gloria hurried to summon servants and refreshment.

'I did not expect to find you here.'

'I'm sure that now you have you are pleasantly surprised.'

June ignored the hard irony in her husband's tone and the frustrated desire that darkened his blue eyes to gleaming jet. She had only recently arrived at Beaulieu Gardens, having sped through Mayfair to convey to Rachel and Isabel Lady Rockingham's invitation. Both had been pleased to receive and accept it.

'It seems you have a hectic programme today.

Shopping with Blackmore this morning and a visit to Lady Rockingham planned for this afternoon. Am I to book an hour of your time to dine later?'

'I welcome keeping busy. I do not want time to think at the moment. I'd far sooner have too little time on my hands than too much.'

There was a pointed reference to their troubles in her answer that froze the air between them.

'Why are you here?' June asked after a short silence.

William shrugged casually, about to say he had just popped in on passing. Instead he settled on telling the truth. 'I came hoping to find you here.'

Immediately June sent him a sharp look. 'Have you some…news for me?' she asked in a low voice that mingled hope and trepidation.

In truth, all the news William had was that he had no news. His efforts to extract the truth from Lady Bingham had been fruitless. But, if he had something to impart, now would not have been the time to do it. He wanted some time alone with his wife away from the constant cautious observation of friends and family.

He shook his head and, because her disappointment made her half-turn away, he sought to keep her there with idle conversation. 'How is my friend Blackmore? Well, I trust? I have not seen him myself for a while.'

'He seems very well,' June replied. 'He sends his best wishes to you.'

'In that case you must convey mine to him. Shall we dine together later?' William asked. A plea was in his eyes, if absent from the lightly spoken enquiry.

'I...I don't know whether I shall be late back from Lady Rockingham's salon. I shall not mind if you do not wait. You might get hungry.' June was very conscious of blue eyes boring into the side of her face.

'I am able to curb my appetite...'

His slow sardonic drawl brought a beautiful blush to accentuate June's high cheekbones. Her head tilted up and her tawny eyes challenged the mocking humour in his face.

'Do you never get hungry, June?'

'Of course I do,' June breathed. 'But a fast can be cleansing...and necessary. Perhaps at some time you might appreciate its benefit.'

'Perhaps I shall...but the memory of a banquet is not easily forgotten. I am human and tempted to seek sustenance.'

'Then eat when you like and with whom...' June hissed.

'Do you mean that?'

June swung back towards him, having angrily backed away a few paces.

'Do you mean that?' William repeated in a growl, his eyes capturing hers.

Simultaneously they became aware that they were drawing attention from the other adults in the room. Only Sylvie seemed oblivious to the tension between her sister and brother-in-law.

June flicked a glance sideways and, with true diplomacy, Adam's eyes shifted effortlessly to his cup and he lifted it to his mouth. It hovered there, tea untasted, as he noticed the seductive *ingenue* was strolling his way. Sylvie halted in front of his chair.

'I am not sure I want to go to your mother's house party, although, of course, it is kind of her to ask me. I imagine those twins Deirdre and Diane Mortimer might be there. They think they're so grand and have planned a flash come-out ball for May.'

Adam's intense appreciation of her exquisite features went uninterrupted, although he managed to tilt his mouth in a mildly sympathetic smile.

'A few of your ladies of doubtful character might be better company.'

That bright observation had the effect of making Lord Malvern choke on a sip of tea. The coughing fit that ensued slopped wet from his cup on to his breeches.

Sylvie tutted concern, found a napkin on the table, and immediately set to mopping up the damage.

As though scalded, Adam shot back in his chair, sending it skidding on the parquet. The teacup clattered on to a table and his long fingers gripped and held rigidly, at arm's length, the small hand clutching a cloth that, seconds before, had been solicitously dabbing his lap.

June and William exchanged a glance of amused horror.

With a slender hand shielding her smile, June murmured, 'I think it is time we got ready to go out.'

'And it is time I took my leave,' William said softly. 'I shall wait dinner for you…till midnight if need be.'

June turned to look at him. 'You will be ravenous by then.'

'I know. I'll wait anyway,' he said.

'I said you would enjoy yourself, young lady,' Gloria happily told her youngest daughter. 'And I believe that Lady Rockingham took a particular shine to you. Those twins were quite put out by it.' Gloria Meredith sank back with a contented smile. It was eight o'clock and coming on to dusk as Gloria, June and Sylvie journeyed home together from Lady Rockingham's salon, having left Isabel and

Rachel to be collected and driven home by their husbands.

'Lady Rockingham seems very nice and the food was delicious,' Sylvie agreed, for in particular she could recall the tiny pastry cases stuffed with sweet and savoury fillings.

'Yes, it was all very tasty.' Gloria hesitated and frowned. 'But I have to say, Sylvie, that you must learn not to partake of the buffet quite so heartily. There is a certain merit in appearing abstemious, especially when in company with the gentlemen. It is not very charming for a young lady to be seen with her jaws constantly chomping and spotted with crumbs.'

'There was so much it seemed a shame to waste it. Besides, there weren't any gentlemen there,' Sylvie reasoned, unperturbed.

'Yes, I know. But on other occasions there will be.'

'I wish that Lord Malvern had been there. I think he likes me.'

'Did he say so?' Gloria demanded after a moment in which she and June had locked eyes.

A reflective frown hovered between her brows as Sylvie cast back her mind. 'Well, I know he keeps company with ladies of doubtful character. I suppose that means they must improve as I must.'

'And how do you know that, pray?' Gloria demanded stiffly, a dangerous maternal glimmer in her eyes.

'I overheard Papa talking to William and Lord Malvern about demi-reps.' She flushed on remembering being rebuked in front of the gentlemen by her papa. 'Papa was cross that I had joined them and wanted me to go away. His lordship was kinder, and satisfied my curiosity. *And* he didn't think I was wrong for wanting to know. *Au contraire*, he said when Papa said I might be thought silly...'

Gloria sent an anxious look at June, for she guessed that what Sylvie had overheard was her husband giving William a dressing down over his visit to a brothel.

As soon as they had had an opportunity to be private, Gloria had learned from Edgar what had prompted their son-in-law's visit to such a dive. She now felt a little guilty at ever having doubted William might not have a proper motive for being spied in such a place. But then he had been accompanied there by one of society's most notorious rakes. It was hardly surprising she had thought the worst.

Edgar had even produced *The Times* newspaper and shown her the paragraph that contained Benjamin Harley's apology to Mr and Mrs William Alexander Pemberton. It was adequate, if imprecise, and had served its purpose. When at Lady Rockingham's several ladies of her acquaintance, who had developed a distinct *froideur* towards her family once the rumours started, had thawed enough to make a point of greeting her warmly. Naturally Gloria had virtually ignored them.

'What was William's contribution to this debate?' June asked her sister in a tight voice.

'Nothing,' Sylvie replied. She wound a pearly curl about a finger. 'William didn't say very much at all. Perhaps there was an argument. I heard Papa shouting, that's why I went to find out what was going on.'

'And this is what happens when people eavesdrop,' Gloria retorted. 'You, young lady, would be well advised to do as you are told. When your father tells you to go away, you must obey him.'

Sylvie's indignant retort that she wasn't eavesdropping and a person in the street could have heard the commotion barely registered with the other occupants in the coach.

'You *knew*,' June accused her mother in a shocked little whisper. 'You and Papa knew that William and that reprobate had been…had been keeping company with harlots.'

'Harlots?'

'Be quiet!' The command issued simultaneously from two voices.

Sylvie shrugged and sighed.

'Do not jump to conclusions, June,' Gloria quietly advised. 'William has explained his reasons to your papa and your papa has told me.' Gloria sighed. 'Please don't ask me to repeat any of it, for I fear I might inadvertently make things worse. Besides, it is your husband's place to tell you. I know all this taken together must be so hard for you to bear, my love.' Gloria's voice was shaky with tears. 'I hate to see you unhappy. William is a good man and lately he looks so terribly sad too.'

'Well, I must not complain then,' June said acidly. 'Perhaps he went there to cheer himself up.'

Chapter Thirteen

'You're home early.'

William's husky welcome brought June to a halt just before one of her dainty slippers stepped onto the bottom tread of the stairs.

'I'm glad to see you. My stomach has been protesting this past hour or more,' he added on a slow teasing smile. 'It was a brave promise I made to wait till midnight. May I tell Herbert that we are ready to dine?'

June turned towards him, unable to speak for the rage of violent emotion that was clogging her throat. She had intended to go straight to bed and avoid a confrontation. Once before at Isabel's home she had used those long, lonely night-time hours to blunt her anger against him and sharpen her reason. She gripped the banister in an attempt to control an urge to speed across the hallway and beat at him with her fists.

'I can wait a little longer. Do you want to refresh yourself before we eat?'

'I want to retire,' June managed to force out in a voice made querulous from distress.

'And I want to take that as an invitation for us both to have an early night.' His affectionate tone was already lost to irony. 'But of course, it isn't.'

He strolled closer and June noted obliquely that he had dressed for dinner with great care. His dark clothes were immaculate, his hard angular cheeks freshly shaven. Her husband looked heartbreakingly handsome and the more conscious of it she became, the more painful was the ache within. She stared at him as though entranced by his presence. Of course, she knew she was envied because she had married well. But why had she never before fully appreciated the thrill of his virility? A nearby sconce flickered, highlighting the silver at his temples to mock her. The idea of another woman tangling her fingers in his hair, tantalising her palm with the rough edge of his jaw, was too much to bear.

She was tortured with images of her husband giving another woman those intimate pleasures that were hers alone. The thought of him with a mistress of some refinement was harrowing; imagining him lying with a common prostitute sent nausea to scald her throat.

Suddenly he was close enough to catch her arm

and prevent her bolting. 'What is the matter?' he asked softly, then grunted a mirthless laugh. 'That was a stupid thing to say. Obviously I know already what is the matter. But…' his eyes scanned her strained face '…there is something else… something new. What is it?'

June tilted her chin and her fierce eyes darted to his. 'Very well, I shall tell you. I am disgusted that you have allowed your friend to speak of loose women with my young sister. She is only sixteen and not yet out. I do not think she needs to have the term demi-rep explained.'

William shoved his hands in his pockets and his head tilted at the ceiling. 'As you know that much, you must also know that your father was present at the time of the incident. Direct your righteous anger at him, not me.'

'That is for my mother to do.'

'I agree. And if your mother has not taken him to task over what occurred, perhaps that is because she knows the full story and is aware of mitigating circumstances. I think Sylvie is not your main concern at all. I think what irks you is not knowing why I was involved in a conversation about demi-reps.'

'I think I can guess the answer to that,' June sweetly snapped. 'Sylvie heard my father shouting when closeted with you and Lord Malvern. I imagine Papa had accused you of keeping company with harlots. Are you about to deny that is why he was angry?'

'No. That is exactly why he was angry.'

A small hand immediately cracked hard on a fleshless cheek. June back-stepped up one stair. 'I am sorry. I should not have done that.' The words vibrated with such fury it made nonsense of the apology. 'I now recall having given you permission today to slake your appetite elsewhere. You obviously guessed earlier in the week that I would do so and lost no time in gorging yourself.'

William simply stared unflinchingly at her with eyes that looked as black as ebony.

His composure simply heightened June's vexation. Suddenly instead of wanting to flee from him, she was determined to stay long enough to prod from him a vehement response. 'You admitted your friend is disreputable. Mr Blackmore has called him a villain too. And you…you will simply say you are human and have succumbed to temptation. Despite your boast earlier, you cannot…will not curb your appetite.'

June gripped the banister and glared at him with tawny eyes that threatened stormy tears. 'Why so quiet? Have you no pathetic defence? No lies to tell me?'

William's smile chilled her heart. 'You are not

sure what has gone on, are you?' he said quietly. 'Yet you would rather believe your overwrought imagination than ask me why I was in a bawdy house with Townsend, and believe what I tell you. What happened to trust and loyalty, June?'

'How dare you try to make *me* feel guilty! Why should I believe what you tell me after all that has gone on?'

'When have I lied to you?'

June swallowed, chewed her lip and frowned. His cold, contained anger was unexpected and unsettling and doubts infiltrated her mind. Her mother had advised her to ask William for his version of events and not jump to conclusions. Her jealousy and pride had made her deaf even to her mother's counsel.

'When have I lied to you?' William bellowed, making her jump and clutch at the spindles for support. 'I imagine Sylvie has innocently repeated to you fragments of an overheard conversation. Would you like me to tell you the rest?'

'I do not for one moment think I could stomach more.' With that hurled defensively over her shoulder, June had twisted about and retreated another step up the stairs when a brawny arm girdled her waist and her husband hauled her back against him.

His lips closed with her small ear, spreading a sensual heat at her nape that made her shiver yet seek its comfort. 'You will listen to this whether you want to or not.' His voice was thick with violent determination. 'I am perhaps guilty of fathering a child out of wedlock, but I am not guilty of adultery or falsehood.' William spun her about and, with her slender wrist manacled by his brutal fingers, pulled her, unwillingly trudging behind him, towards the dining-room door. 'Come, sweet, let me show you what benefit I got from visiting that whorehouse. Then you may go alone to bed.'

The magnificent walnut table that spanned more than twelve feet was set for two to dine cosily close together. Crystal and silver glittered in firelight; shiny china reflected shapes like ghostly morsels. William snatched from the table *The Times*, then sent it skidding along the polished wood towards her. 'Harley has gazetted an apology to us for *any misunderstandings that could be misconstrued as slanderous*—I think those are the weasel words he employs. He agreed to do it when at a distinct disadvantage: Townsend and I had found him naked in his doxy's bed. I don't feel the slightest remorse at having humiliated him into giving his word to make this public announcement. What I do regret is not having chosen a better time and place to browbeat him.'

June looked at the paper and then at her husband.

William managed half a sardonic smile. 'Take it

with you. A little bedtime reading might delay your slumber, but never fear that I will.'

June picked up the paper in quivering fingers. She was being summarily dismissed, but her indignation was swallowed by shame. Her husband's wrath wound about her like a stifling cocoon until it seemed too late to salve her conscience with a few conciliatory words.

With her head high but her voice low, June quickly called to William before he could quit the room. 'If I have judged you harshly, I'm sorry. I hate to be suspicious, but there is so much horrible uncertainty. All I yearn for is an end to not knowing.'

'Not so very long ago all you yearned for was my baby,' William returned in a voice that was harshly melancholic. The door closed quietly as he left.

If many a true word was spoken in jest, the same philosophy could apply to words launched in anger. With that maxim circling her weary head, June rose unrefreshed from her jumbled bed. Pulling back the heavy curtains she watched with wistful entrancement as the dawn became a blush on the horizon. For an unknown reason, and one she was too exhausted to investigate, the flamboyant view settled on her a calm determination to put an end to not knowing...

As soon as a reasonable hour to visit approached, June donned her most stylish walking gown and went out alone without her maid, Verity, accompanying her. She walked some streets away before hailing a hackney cab and instructing the driver to take her to Belgravia.

'Will you take tea?'

'I thank you, no.'

Constance Bingham shifted her shoulders. It was an approximation of a shrug intended to convey her indifference. An elegant white finger indicated a gilt-framed chair. 'Please sit down, Mrs Pemberton.'

'Thank you.' June's polite acceptance sounded as aloof as had the offer.

As she settled herself June was peripherally conscious she was being subjected to a discreet appraisal. Her chin flicked up and she boldly invited her hostess's inspection.

Lady Bingham blinked and looked away, but not quickly enough to conceal the glint of jealousy narrowing her eyes.

A month or so ago such an explicit display of rivalry from this woman might have toppled June's confidence. Now she simply felt irritated and emboldened enough by it to immediately open proceedings. The sooner she might discover the truth and thus return home the better she would like it. 'I must thank you for receiving me without a prior appointment.'

Lady Bingham graciously inclined her head, acknowledging that indeed it was a generosity on her part.

There was a subtle slight in the gesture that was not lost on June. If the woman thought she might cow her with a superior attitude, she was mistaken. Constance Bingham might be the daughter of a baronet and the widow of an earl…she might even have once been William's chosen wife, but June had so far detected nothing other than unpleasantness in this woman's character. She would not despise Constance for deviating from society's constraints and losing her maidenhood before marriage. Perhaps it had been a selfless act of love for William, or perhaps it had been seduction…

Quickly June drove away such painful thoughts and concentrated on the woman's more recent aberrations. She had certainly made an unseemly spectacle of her interest in a married man. It was hardly conduct of which to be proud. With that thought bolstering her determination, June again attempted to start a conversation.

'There is no point in making any pretence over

the reason for my visit, Lady Bingham. You must know I am not here to curry friendship. I am sure you are also aware that objectionable gossip is circulating concerning the Binghams and the Pembertons. The point of my visit is to ascertain whether you will assist us in putting an end to the rumours once and for all.'

June paused, giving the woman an opportunity to comment. Constance Bingham simply lifted her teacup to her delicately rouged lips. June had her suspicions confirmed by gleaming eyes insolently challenging her. Constance Bingham was glad… triumphant that her name was being linked with William's.

'As the gossip concerns your child I imagine you must be greatly angered by it. I'm sure I would be,' June reasoned mildly. She stripped off a glove and let the supple leather fall to her lap.

Constance put down her cup. 'Then you must be glad your temper will ever remain unprovoked, Mrs Pemberton. I understand William still has no *male* heir…' The sarcasm was purred at June and Constance lowered her eyes and allowed a tiny sly smile to tug at her lips.

June felt the blood rise in her cheeks, but swallowed her ire. She was more annoyed at herself for having stupidly uttered something that would make her vulnerable to such an attack.

'Naturally I am concerned for my daughter's well-being,' Constance continued while rhythmically smoothing her satin skirts with the backs of her fingers. 'I cherish her and am glad she is too young and too far away to be affected by any malice. When she is old enough I will disclose to her those important facts she ought know.'

'Which are?' June immediately regretted that her impatience to cut to the chase and gain some proper answers had made her sound impertinent.

Lady Bingham cocked her head and her amusement skewed her mouth into a vermilion slash. 'Do not look so crestfallen, Mrs Pemberton. I understand that inquisitiveness can make people act indecorously. With an empty nursery yourself it must be galling for you to hear it said that your husband has a child with his first love.'

'I have not come here either for pity or for scorn,' June said with quiet pride. 'Neither have I come to defend or to accuse my husband. The rumour is thus far unsubstantiated. You were the wife of a well-respected gentleman. I imagined that you would want to scotch insinuations about your child's father to honour your husband's memory. I have come to discuss how matters can be made better for all concerned. That is my purpose in visiting you.'

'I think you are only concerned for yourself, Mrs

Pemberton. I think that because you are childless you want to persuade me to deny how intimately I once knew your husband, simply so you might save face.'

'Are you saying that my husband sired your daughter?' June immediately whipped back in a whisper.

'I am saying that if I were to discuss such a delicate matter, then I would naturally do so with the person who is central to the drama...*not* with his wife.'

June felt an icy embarrassment needle her skin. Yesterday her husband had summarily dismissed her from his presence. Today it was the turn of his—what was Lady Bingham to him? Forgotten fiancée? Mother of his child? Nothing at all? June felt her stomach heaving in anguish as she realised she simply didn't know.

'I am aware of your straitened circumstances, Lady Bingham, and I am sorry for you, but if you think to fuel these lies simply to find in my husband a meal ticket, you will be sadly disappointed. He is a gentleman, not a fool.' June gained her feet. 'I will waste no more of my time, Lady Bingham, and bid you good day.'

'Past folly can come back to haunt one...as your husband now knows. But do not look so anxious, Mrs Pemberton.' Constance's light tone could not disguise that June's frosty speech had affected her deeply. Her powder-pale complexion was burning bright spots of colour high on each cheek. 'William has been keen to keep in contact with me. He was here earlier this week.' Constance announced this with a fierce triumph that tightened the pit of June's stomach and persuaded her it was true. 'Soon the time will be right for him to tell you the truth about us.'

'You are lying!' June said in a low, vibrant voice. 'William will never let an unfortunate liaison in his youth come between us. He has said so.'

'I would expect no less of him. He was ever gentlemanlike.' Constance's tone hinted at a husky sneer. 'It is amazing, is it not, that beneath his sobriety is a man of such…energetic passion? Perhaps a virtuous little madam like you has no lover…no comparison to make. But I have comparisons, so many… Believe me when I say that William is hard to forget…hard to forgo… Everything about him is so hard…hard…hard…'

'Good day.' June struggled blindly to find the doorknob, struggled to block out the sound of lewd laughter that accompanied her into the marble-flagged hallway. It was only when she was close to the noble portal of the house that her temper surfaced from beneath the shock of being subjected to such coarse talk. Lady Bingham, widow of an earl, a member of polite society, had just acted like the wanton June had suspected her to be. Suddenly June was bedevilled by an urgent need to race back and tell the woman how vile she thought her. She didn't succumb to the urge to act as vulgarly as had her tormentor and, in her eagerness to breathe clean air, barely acknowledged the aged butler who politely held the door for her.

The fresh morning air cooled the sprinkling of warm tears on June's cheeks and, once aware of the moisture, she dashed it away. After taking a deep, calming breath, she scoured the street for a hackney to take her home. She spied one at the junction with Waverley Street, but it pulled away from the kerb with a new fare before she had taken more than a half-dozen paces in that direction.

June spun about and noticed that, almost opposite the townhouse from which she had recently fled, another vehicle had stopped to allow a portly lady to alight. She hurriedly retraced her steps, hoping to secure a ride back to St James's.

She stood on the pavement, staring at the elegant façade of that hateful house which was visible through the windows of the cab, deaf to the demands of the driver. Eventually his raucous impatience penetrated her shock and she glanced up at his weatherbeaten countenance. June managed to shake her head, simultaneously shrinking back into the shadow of a budding lime tree.

As the conveyance pulled away she had an interrupted view of the distinguished gentleman she had just spied mounting the steps she had so recently descended. He was now rapping on the door while looking about. Suddenly he threw back his head, stared up at the sky as though impatient for admittance.

The elderly butler opened the door and then the lady of the house was there too. June watched, her face a chalky mask, her bone-white knuckles grazing the trunk of the tree as Constance Bingham stepped on to the stone step and promptly slid her arms about William's neck and kissed him.

Chapter Fourteen

'What the hell do you think you are about?'

The rebuke was gritted out with tooth-shattering ferocity as William strode through the door with Lady Bingham still an appendage. He removed her limpet fingers from his neck and immediately put distance between them.

'I do not know what game you think you are playing, madam, but I have not come here for you to make a public spectacle of us. Why did you insist I come in person rather than send me a letter? Was it simply so you might throw yourself at my head on your doorstep and thus incite more gossip?'

The butler had closed the double doors and was now hovering. The elderly servant had been in Lady Bingham's employ only the few months since she came up from Devon for the season. In his prime he had presided over far grander vestibules, and taken far better remuneration. Never, in all his years of service, had he witnessed a lady act quite so outrageously and he hoped that, for the pittance the hussy had persuaded him to accept, she was not expecting his duties to include ejecting gentlemen who didn't appreciate her being shockingly amorous. A wary glance scanned the muscular frame of the vexed fellow and he shrank into his shoes.

'Go about your duties, my good man,' William instructed quite kindly, having noticed the manservant's uneasy stance. Without waiting for his employer to sanction his dismissal the butler gratefully hobbled away. William's attention reverted to the brunette sullenly peeping at him from beneath a web of dark eyelashes. 'Lead on to somewhere private where we might talk.'

That snapped command elicited a petulant look, but Constance swished about and, hips undulating with every step, glided to a nearby door.

Once within the room, where a short while before she had received this man's wife, Constance turned to William. A scornful stare met her bold invitation and she put a hand to her throat as though to stay the rash of colour spreading there. 'I beg you will not be angry with me, William. I…I could not control myself just now. I did not want to simply pen a letter. I have yearned to see you.'

William slung her a frown of disbelief. 'You

have *yearned* to see me?' he echoed. 'Why? You have seen me often enough. My wife and I were recent guests at Lord Malvern's party. You were also present and we exchanged pleasantries.'

'Pleasantries? I do not want pleasantries! You must know why I have wanted to meet you privately,' Constance cried huskily. 'I have never managed to put from my mind the incredible passion we shared. I know there is gossip about us. I do not wonder at it. My mourning is finally at an end. People have remembered that once we were in love. We were to be married, but stupidly I listened to my family instead of my heart…'

'What nonsense is this?' William interrupted on a brusque laugh. 'You are harking back to events that occurred a long time ago when we were both adolescents. You chose someone else and I married a woman I adore. I'll allow that there is gossip about us and also that once we were betrothed. But that is all that is honest in what you have said.' He paused and looked at her for the first time with a modicum of sympathy. 'I can only imagine you are prey to loneliness and nostalgia now Charlie Bingham is gone.'

'It is nothing to do with him!' A contemptuous flick of a hand dismissed her late husband as inconsequential. 'But there was something between *us*…we were lovers,' Constance insisted, a glitter hardening her eyes.

'Our relationship was misguided…a *mésalliance*.' William's tone made it clear he deemed her attitude absurd. 'Had we gone on to marry we both would have been dissatisfied with our lot.'

'I would not! You satisfied me more than any other man I have known. I cannot forget that wonderful occasion when you proved so many times how much you desired me—'

'This is madness.' William curtly cut across her explicit flattery. He strode to the door as if he would leave. 'I think, madam, you are deluded and ought seek the help of a physician. Perhaps you are afflicted with melancholy.'

'I am afflicted with a broken heart,' Constance called theatrically. 'Why will you not admit that there was something between us?'

'Very well, if you insist on candour, I concede there was something between us,' William drawled in irritation. 'Lust.'

Constance hurried after him as he jerked the door ajar. 'Are you going? Before we have discussed my daughter? From your letters I know you suspect that you sired Cissy.'

William shut the door again and with straining patience turned back to her. 'Then I'm sorry my prose can be misconstrued,' he returned in a weary tone. 'By my recollection I implied nothing of the sort. I asked you to confirm that the rumours, not the child, were spurious. I am still awaiting your response. You must have known your reticence would incite more speculation.' William narrowed his eyes on a downcast face. 'I am here now, willing to listen. Still you seem reluctant to be specific.' He paused, allowing her time to rectify matters and finally tell him what he wanted to know.

Constance bowed her head and dabbed at her face with a scrap of lace.

'Damnation! I believe you are a good enough actress to tread the boards at Drury Lane.' The chuckle that scratched at William's throat was nearly amused. 'There will be no more letters and no more visits. Do not contact me again except through my lawyers. With or without your help I hope to soon bring an end to this farce. I have sent private investigators to Devon.'

'What do you mean by that?' Constance dropped her handkerchief away from her flawless complexion and sent him a sharp look.

'I thought that news might dry your tears,' William said sardonically. 'Not to put too fine a point on it, madam, when we consummated our betrothal it was obvious to me, even at a tender age, that it was not the first time you had bestowed your favours. I would wager a tidy sum that even before the engagement was broken you had other lovers. I had no illusions about you then. I am certainly not about to be gulled now. In short, I know there are other candidates for the deed.' William smiled inwardly at the calculation narrowing her eyes as she endeavoured to guess his intentions. 'I accept that the child might not be your late husband's, for it was rumoured Charlie might lack in that respect…'

Constance's lips slanted in sly disappointment. 'He was of no use at all in that respect.'

'But you soon found someone who was. Are his pockets to let? Is that why you have come up to town? To find a sap willing to bail out your swain now you can no longer do so yourself?'

Constance swiftly averted her face, but not before William had glimpsed her dismay. He paced back into the room. 'My God,' he said slowly. 'That is it, isn't it? You hoped to play on my conscience and attempt to extort money from me to give to him. In which case I assume this pathetic attempt at blackmail is your work.' He withdrew from a pocket the note he had received and thrust it at her.

Constance scanned the script and frowned. A scoffing smile turned down her lips, but there was a wary look haunting her eyes. 'You can't seriously think I would bother with such a paltry sum?' She flicked the note back at him. 'If it was my work I would have demanded ten times as much.'

'Yes, I must admit that had occurred to me,' William drawled damningly.

Constance peered at him over an arrogantly elevated shoulder. 'You are a fool to reject me because of that barren mouse you married. I did not expect you to divorce her. In fact, I have no desire to again be a wife. I am a far better mistress. Are you sure you do not want a little sample of the ecstasy you miss?'

William simply stared at her, his eyes brimming with disgust.

Constance brazenly came closer and circled him. Suddenly a white finger was raised and a sharp nail tickled one of his cheeks.

William disdainfully flicked his head to one side at the same moment Constance drew blood. She backed away, smirking. 'Go! Go away…explain my brand to your sweet little wife.'

William put a hand to the thin welt on his cheek. 'God help your daughter if she favours you,' was all William muttered as he quit the room.

Lady Bingham mouthed an obscenity at the closed door and her simmering anger erupted, manifesting in her hurling to the floor the closest ornament to hand.

She then flew over the broken shards of porcelain to a small desk in the corner and scribbled a note. The bell was rung with violence until her butler, in a limping gait, arrived to find out what was causing the commotion. 'An urgent letter to be hand delivered,' she snapped at him. 'Quick! Do it now, you goggling old fool!'

'I want to talk to you, June.'

June froze momentarily to the spot with a hand on the banister, and a foot hovering over a tread. Quickly she resumed her graceful descent of the sweeping curve of stairs. 'It must wait. I cannot stop now,' she breathed with barely a tremor to her voice. 'I am on my way out…a prior engagement with Gavin…Mr Blackmore.' *William had something to tell her.* In her mind's eyes June could see the gloating look in the eyes of that preying widow as she had crowed, *'Soon the time will be right for him to tell you the truth about us.'*

Earlier that afternoon she had been so anguished by the scene she had witnessed between her husband and Lady Bingham that, had William soon come upon her she might have succumbed to hysteria or aggression. But, of course, she'd had no need to fret her husband might soon be home. She had no need to guess why he had been so long abroad or how he and Lady Bingham might have occupied their time together. If the woman were confident enough of her allure to blatantly kiss him on her front step, once within doors she would have still fewer inhibitions. Perhaps it was during pillow talk that she had persuaded William that his wife should be told about the two of them.

Had Constance Bingham regaled William with all that had gone on when his wife had called earlier in the day? Would he take her to task over that? June knew she should confront William, but she could not. She felt unprepared to deal with the anguish he might inflict on her. Her husband seemed increasingly to be a stranger to her, yet still the thought of losing his love was unendurable.

June gasped in a silent sob of a breath and steadied herself with the banister. She must not jump to conclusions, she inwardly impressed on herself. She must not allow hurt and humiliation to give rise to feverish imaginings. There might be a reasonable explanation why a vulgar wanton had kissed and embraced her husband in public.

This time there were no malicious tongues to blame for inventing a scandal. It was a truth she had witnessed and could not deny. She came down the few remaining stairs. She knew she must get away for a while. A little distraction might help her until she could be sure of controlling her emotions enough to discuss matters reasonably.

William caught at his wife's arm as she made to slip past him on her way to the street door. Blue eyes slowly looked her up and down. 'It is the first time I have seen you wear that outfit. As I recall, it was put away in your clothes' press because you did not like it.'

June glanced down at a fitted bodice of flimsy peach muslin that was scooped quite daringly low across her breasts. An equally light skirt floated tantalisingly about her body with little more than a cobweb of underskirt veiling lissom limbs.

'I have not worn it before,' June answered with some asperity, walking backwards while speaking to him. 'When first I had it made, I regretted it. I did not think it fitting. Now I have changed my mind. I think I do like it and it suits me very well.'

William stalked her retreat, while passing a lazy gaze over her revealingly attired lush little figure. 'It is not very clement today. Do you think you ought go abroad in nothing more than a camisole and petticoat to spare your blushes and keep you warm?'

William took her cloak from her grip and settled it with slow sensuality about her slender shoulders.

'Oh, this cloak is wool and I shan't blush, William.'

June felt her husband's hands tighten on the fastening under her chin. She cocked her head, her whole demeanour challenging his restraint. Soon her expression softened, for her eyes were drawn to the scratch on his cheek. With instinctive frowning concern one of her hands was soon raising to soothe it. Within a hair's breadth of his skin her outstretched fingers shrank into her palm. 'You have had an accident…' she murmured.

William rubbed the mark with a careless finger. 'It is nothing…nothing at all.' He looked at the small fist close to his face. 'Are you intending to add to the damage?'

William immediately regretted the remark as he saw his wife's eyes dart back to the wound. The expression in her soulful eyes had changed from sympathy to suspicion. With his unwitting help she had recognised it for what it was: a woman's brand. 'We need to talk, June. It is important,' William cajoled throatily.

So sadly sure was June that they were pondering on the same person at that precise moment that she choked out, 'I have no time and no inclination to discuss Lady Bingham with you.' Within a moment she had freed herself and passed him.

'How have you been, my dear? Well, I trust? It is *so* nice to meet you unexpectedly.'

June looked curiously at the person who had greeted her. The woman was not a stranger, but her affable attitude was definitely foreign.

June and Mr Blackmore had just been on the point of taking a stroll about the lake in Hyde Park to talk of his sister's plight when a smart carriage drew alongside and one of the occupants hailed them.

'It is good to see you too, ma'am,' June told her mother-in-law while wondering curiously why she now pleased Pamela Pemberton.

June tilted her head, including her father-in-law in her cordial smile. Alexander returned her a courteous nod whilst fiddling with the carriage ribbons. Conscious that William's parents were not intending to immediately move on, June continued politely, if not wholly truthfully, 'William and I have lately missed seeing you. We expected you might attend the *musicale*…'

'We have not been out very much at all,' Pamela disclosed, with a pointed look at her husband.

Alexander missed his wife's wordless rebuke, for he had politely responded to Mr Blackmore's comment on the fresh weather they were experiencing.

'Shall we take a stroll to the lake while the gentlemen have a chat?'

June nodded, while still puzzling over what might have prompted this unexpected bonhomie. June's bemusement escalated as Pamela linked their arms in a cosy fashion.

They had barely gone a few yards towards the water when Pamela sighed. 'It won't do! I must eat humble pie while I think I can.'

June slanted her a look of frank enquiry.

'I have wanted to visit you at home,' Pamela started her explanation. 'But Alexander would not allow it. He said I must stay away in case I caused trouble between you and William. He does not trust me, you know. See! He watches me now...' Pamela hissed, peering over her shoulder.

June obediently turned her head as she received a light dig in the ribs reminding her to check on their audience. Alexander Pemberton indeed appeared to be observing them rather than giving Gavin Blackmore his attention.

'He fears I might meddle, even though I have promised not to! You would think, would you not, that after more than three decades wed he would trust me to my word.' Pamela's wide-eyed look begged an ally.

June kindly returned a neutral smile.

'I have told him of my regrets, but he blames me still. He implies it is partly my fault that you and William seem at odds.'

At her mother-in-law's muffled tone, June inclined her head to look beneath Pamela's bonnet brim. She spied downcast eyes and a nose ready to drip. 'I concede that in the past I might have seemed...cool to you. It was simply a disappointment I felt that William's first engagement came to nothing.' Pamela snuffled. 'Only now do I realise it was a double blessing that he was jilted and then was fortunate enough to marry you.'

June swallowed, about to speak, but found she could not immediately think of a single thing to say. This, then, was her apology for the several years of poor treatment she had received at her mother-in-law's hands. Not so long ago she might have felt indignant that it had been so long in coming and was so inadequately delivered. Now, with far greater troubles occupying her mind, she simply squeezed her mother-in-law's arm in comfort and murmured, 'Do not distress yourself, ma'am.'

'I thought Constance genteel and charming…but she is not,' Pamela finished on a hiss, her eyes and lips tightening. 'I have it on good authority that the woman is a scheming hussy. She has been left a pauper by Lord Bingham and it serves her right.' Pamela barely paused before continuing, 'She is not at all the lady I believed her to be. She would have humiliated our son by marrying him when already she had—'

June was sent an intensely meaningful stare that sent Pamela's head to one side and her eyebrows winging into her hairline. 'It is outrageous! When I think that she might have tried to pass off a bastard as our grandchild! You understand my meaning, don't you?'

June knew exactly what her mother-in-law

meant. It was why she felt an urge to mention that just this afternoon Lady Bingham had yet again been acting the scheming hussy with their son. June simply nodded.

Pamela took a glance through misty vision at her daughter-in-law's tense features. 'You must not let that…that creature come between you and William. You are right for him…demure and ladylike…' The flimsy skirt floating about June's ankles received an inspection. 'That is a pretty gown you have on, my dear. It is…unlike the style you usually favour… Oh, look! Alexander is on his way to take me away lest I upset you. I have not upset you, June, have I? He will scold me if I have.'

'No,' June reassured her. 'You have not upset me at all, ma'am.'

'He seems pleasant…'

'What? Who?' June asked on a frown.

'Mr Blackmore.' A nod of the head indicated June's escort. 'He seems nice, but it is being noticed that you have spent a lot of time with him lately and very little with your husband.' Pamela squeezed her arm. 'Now we are friends I know you will not mind me saying so, for it was brought to my attention by Phyllis Chamberlain.' Pamela sniffed derisively. 'Of course, I told her to mind her own business, even if she is your father's sister. But I thought I would just mention it to you…

'Why, Alexander, I was just saying to June that we have missed seeing her and William. It is time, is it not, we had a little get-together?'

'Yes…' Alexander said without enthusiasm. 'Come, my dear, it is time we started home, for I think it is coming on to rain.'

'Nonsense!' Pamela contradicted. 'It is but a cloud.'

'It seems we are not to have an opportunity to talk of your sister today,' June mentioned wryly to Gavin as she waved at her in-laws departing, and then at some newcomers drawing up in a different coach.

'There is nothing good to report in any case,' Gavin responded flatly.

June frowned and slipped him a small bag of coins. She shook her head as he made to protest. 'William makes me a very generous allowance. It is only money I might have spent on fripperies. I would sooner you put it to good use. Come and say hello to my mother. And Sylvie is with her. She is my youngest sister. I shall introduce you to her.'

'We were just taking the pretty route home with our purchases,' was Gloria Meredith's answer to June's enquiry as to what brought them into the park. 'Sylvie has chosen some rather fine Brussels lace to edge the pink muslin Madam Bouillon is making up.' Gloria looked at her youngest daughter for a comment.

Sylvie simply jumped down from the landau to stroke Mr Blackmore's horses. 'Is this your phaeton?' she asked him.

'Alas, no,' he said on a rueful smile. 'I have borrowed it from a friend of mine.'

Sylvie was peering in at the hint of a spring poking through cracked leather upholstery. 'Have you seen Lord Malvern's grand curricle?' she asked.

'Oh, indeed,' Gavin replied drily.

'I would have liked a ride in it.'

'It is mean of him not to oblige you,' Gavin said.

'I think so, too,' Sylvie agreed with a firm nod.

'Manners, Sylvie!' Gloria chided. 'Come, it is time to get along home. You have a fitting with Madam Bouillon.'

At Sylvie's glum look, June and Gavin exchanged a glance. 'We shall give Sylvie a ride about the park in the phaeton and bring her home shortly,' June said, with a smile of thanks directed Gavin's way.

Sylvie beamed at her mother and got a heavy sigh in return.

'Oh, very well. But don't be an age, young lady. Here, give me the bag with the lace.'

'Look!' Sylvie exclaimed as Gavin helped her

alight. 'Lord Malvern is over there! I expect that is a demi-rep with him.'

June choked on an embarrassed chuckle. 'Sylvie! That is Lady Forsythe. She is very nice.'

'It is an easy mistake to make where Townsend is concerned,' Gavin muttered before proceeding to show Sylvie how one must hold the reins.

June stepped over to speak to Adam Townsend and Lady Forsythe.

'I see your sister is already drawing admirers.' Adam watched Gavin Blackmore threading reins in and out of small, graceful fingers. 'I seem out of favour with her today,' he added ruefully on noticing Sylvie had barely glanced his way.

'That is because you have not taken her for a ride in your curricle.' June included Lady Forsythe in her wry smile. 'My young sister can be fickle-hearted as well as adorable.'

'Ah, sisters!' the middle-aged dowager said on a knowledgeable nod. 'I have one and *she* can be a trial! But I must not complain for I would not want to be without her. That poor gentleman must miss his sister dreadfully.'

June glanced warily at Lady Forsythe. 'You know about Bethany Blackmore?' she asked hesitantly.

'My sister knew of their family, oh, some many

years ago now, when she lived in Devon. I understood the girl was named Laura, but I might be mistaken. Perhaps that was the mother's name. But it is a shame the youngster died.'

Chapter Fifteen

'Died?' June's astonishment was gruff with disbelief.

She glanced at Adam for his reaction, but he was engaged with a lady and her daughter who had succeeded, on their second stroll by, to catch his attention.

'Diphtheria...or perhaps it was smallpox... I cannot now recall for my sister told me about it a long time ago.' Lady Forsythe started to nod her head in sympathy. Suddenly she stuck out a hand to test the air. 'Come along, Townsend! Get us moving! It is starting to rain. My new style will suffer, you know.' Her elaborate coiffure received an anxious pat.

Adam suavely saluted the disappointed ladies. June received from him a genuine smile. Finally, with a frown Sylvie's way, he sent his coal-black stallions into a trot.

A slow spatter of raindrops began dotting black into the blue silk of June's cloak; still she stood dazed by what she had heard. Sylvie's laughter finally broke through her confusion and brought her back to the phaeton.

Gavin was pulling up the creaky hood with Sylvie's eager assistance. As June joined her on the seat her sister, still giggling, covered their laps with a travelling rug.

Gavin was breathing hard from the exertion of forcing into position the dilapidated rain cover when the pouch of coins June had given him dropped from his pocket with a chink. Sylvie picked it up, rattled the money, then made to mischievously hide it behind her back. Immediately the purse was snatched from her and stuffed back whence it came.

Gavin's eyes met June's and for a moment his impenitent scowl frightened her. The questions she had been ready to put to him, about what she had heard concerning his family and Bethany in particular, withered on her lips.

Within a moment Gavin was smiling with his usual diffident charm. 'That was rather rude of me,' he mildly apologised. 'I must get you both home before I am in trouble with your family. William will ring a peal over my head if either one of you catches a chill from being out in this weather.'

Neither June nor Sylvie responded, for both were still shocked by his spontaneous boorishness. Just moments before he had been acting the impeccable gallant.

'And you must be home in time for your seamstress's visit.' Gavin persevered in his attempt to restore an air of harmony. A casual look slanted up at the leaden skies. 'I think it will be quite a downpour.'

Sylvie was unimpressed by his smooth talk and glared reproachfully at him. 'It was just a game. I would not steal from you, you know,' she muttered and slid along the seat towards June.

'Of course; I am sorry,' Gavin muttered. Being reminded of his incivility clearly irritated him, but, as though in an effort to finally banish the episode, he offered, 'Would you like to drive a short distance? I shall help you handle the ribbons.'

Sylvie shook her head and instead tossed her face to the driving rain. A flicker of resentment tightened Gavin's features despite his easy shrug. He made to whip leather over the horses' backs; instead, the reins fell slack.

Increasingly uneasy, June searched about to see the reason for the delay. She was regretting having suggested taking Sylvie for a ride in the phaeton and had a powerful instinct to quickly get her young sister safely home. She soon spotted that Mr Blackmore was staring at a youth weaving a path towards them whilst keeping beneath the dripping trees to shelter from the worst of the rain.

The young fellow, on spying the phaeton, ran the few remaining yards to the vehicle whilst jamming his hat protectively low on his brow. He thrust up a note and, once it was taken, left his expectant palm extended. His reward was only terse thanks. The youth slunk off, a sullen stare slung back at them.

'He is my landlady's son. A surly enough fellow if ever there was one.'

Gavin's excuse for his meanness did nothing to alleviate June's disquiet. 'It must be an urgent message for him to come out looking for you to deliver it.' She barely paused before adding, 'Let us quickly get Sylvie back to Beaulieu Gardens, please. My mother will be worrying about her.'

June's eyes darted here and there, assessing the environment. The park was emptying of carriages now the rain had properly set in. A few promenaders who had lingered under the trees, expecting the shower to pass, had given up that hope and were dashing away to find better cover. She fidgeted on the seat. 'Mr Blackmore, we must go!' she implored.

June's demand had little effect. Gavin did not look up from breaking the seal on his note. A low, driven oath followed a perusal of its contents. June felt Sylvie slip her hand through her arm and hug closer. Her young sister was not of a nervous disposition, but was obviously also sensing a queer atmosphere.

The letter was stuffed into a pocket. Catching up the reins, Gavin sent them snaking over horseflesh. His swift sideways glance took in June's fretful expression. A boyish smile ensued, but June was not tempted to feel reassured. She suddenly understood that the careful attention she had been used to receiving from this man was not so much born of his interest, but his calculation. As though seeing him properly for the first time, she realised he was gauging her reaction so he might adapt his own.

'I must beg your pardon if I have seemed short-tempered, but I have been most anxious to receive that communication. I expect you have realised the letter is from Bethany.' It was the same grave tone he always used when speaking of his poor sister. 'It has got speedily to me via my landlady's kindness, for she knew I waited on it. Unfortunately, it confirms what I suspected, but dreaded knowing. Bethany writes that she is ill again. I must purchase some laudanum for her with the money you have kindly donated. I cannot bear to think of her discomfort.'

June did not reply as they proceeded from the

park, for her mind was in turmoil. She was glad they were at last on the way home, yet depressed that what had seemed a pleasant interlude in an unpleasant day was actually turning into nothing of the sort. Again her thoughts circled back to what Lady Forsythe had said.

If Mr Blackmore's sister was dead from disease, how could she write to him from gaol complaining of feeling ill? It seemed absurd to suppose that Bethany might be a fictitious character in a plot Gavin Blackmore had concocted. But June felt compelled to discover whether the gentleman she had considered a friend considered her a gullible fool, who would simply swallow whichever yarns he fed her. Was he really so desperate for her sovereigns that he would stoop so low to get them? He had certainly made it clear that the money she donated was important to him by so churlishly snatching it from Sylvie's hand. Indignation prompted her to blurt out her suspicions.

'I fear that something is not right, Mr Blackmore. I have heard an odd tale that your sister died of an illness many years ago. If that is so, how can Bethany now be incarcerated in the Fleet?'

Gavin didn't even turn his head to look at her. His profile looked skeletally tight and so clumsily did he steer past a lumbering cart that the trio were jerked sideways by his ineptitude. Unbelievably, once round the obstruction, he urged the horses to a greater pace. June struggled to find her balance on the precarious seat and pulled Sylvie protectively close.

Finally, when the vehicle was racketing along straight, if not safe, Gavin uttered in a tone of sombre resignation, 'It is a shame. I had hoped that things might come good for me before you found out. Who told you? I know it was not your husband or Townsend. My fellow scholars knew little of my home life. I made sure of that.' He turned her way and June noticed that the fall of light brown hair over his eyes was darkly sleek with rain. Tear-like rivulets ran down his cheeks. 'You are fortunate, Mrs Pemberton. You have lived a charmed life. You have no idea, have you, what it is like to be without, to be deprived of what others, less entitled, take for granted?'

June ignored his self-pity and said coldly, 'It does not matter how I have found out. Why on earth would you fabricate such a tale? If you have striven to keep your past a secret, I imagine everything else that you disclosed to me about your parents and so on is a lie, too.' June was no longer interested in his reply for she had become peripherally aware that something else was wrong. 'Where are we going?' she demanded as she noticed they had turned towards the suburbs rather than towards Mayfair.

'Take us to Beaulieu Gardens immediately,' she ordered.

When he made no reply, but sent the horses into a perilous canter on the glistening cobbles, June lunged at the reins. Gavin elbowed her roughly off and growled, 'Sit still, Mrs Pemberton. I warn you to sit still! Do as you are told and you will come to no harm.'

'Take me home, you brute!' Sylvie, squashed between them, immediately took over attempting to grapple the reins from Gavin's grasp, and added a fairly hefty punch or two to his shoulder for good measure.

'Stop this carriage at once and put us down,' June yelled breathlessly, restraining Sylvie lest she got injured.

'I can't do that, I'm afraid. You know too much and are thus a liability...unless I can discover some value in you...' His eyes half-closed in consideration and a crafty smile suddenly tilted his mouth.

June cuddled Sylvie to her, stroking away straggly silver tresses from her rain-damp face. 'I beg you will listen to me! Let us take Sylvie home and I shall remain with you,' she reasoned desperately, yet in a voice shrill with panic.

The plea earned her nothing other than a derisive laugh. 'I really would be a dolt to agree to that! Do not try to humour me, Mrs Pemberton. I am not a madman, rather a desperate man who is infinitely ambitious…'

June leaned forward, watching slick grey ground spinning past.

'I would not attempt it. But it is your choice whether you jump and break your neck,' Gavin mocked. 'But then I don't imagine you would risk leaving this comely maiden at my tender mercy…'

Gavin turned a lascivious eye on her young sister. June instinctively enclosed Sylvie in a fierce protective embrace that sought to shield her from his view. To distract him, June asked desperately, 'Why are you doing this? Why have you lied and invented someone called Bethany?'

'I have not invented someone called Bethany. You asked to meet her, did you not? I am an obliging soul, Mrs Pemberton. I shall take you to meet Bethany.'

Sylvie struggled free of June's restraint. 'I'm not going with you! I hate you! Take me home!' she shouted and let fly with a small fist. The blow landed with a crunch just behind one of Gavin's ears, wobbling him on the seat. Without hesitation he instantly retaliated. A short jab to Sylvie's chin rendered her immediately unconscious. June supported her gracefully crumpling form, preventing her from falling.

'You vile beast!' June screamed as they thundered on and swerved east so the driving rain slanted further beneath the hood to drench them. 'Stop and put us down now. Or I swear I shall jump.'

Gavin put back his head and guffawed. 'Go ahead and jump, if you dare. You can't carry your sister and you certainly won't leave her with me, I'm sure of that. I got no enjoyment from hitting the sweet innocent, but she would certainly provide other pleasure...'

June's face became chalky and her arms tightened about Sylvie's limp form. What he'd said was infuriatingly true. She could probably escape herself, should she dare to risk life and limb. But how on earth could she leave Sylvie behind?

'They are dead in a ditch, I know it!'

Edgar Meredith rocked his hysterical wife in his arms and whispered soothingly to her but his face, visible across her shuddering shoulders, was ashen. 'I shall just go and see if William is back with any news. Sit here by the fire...' He led Gloria, tottering on nerve-racked legs, towards an armchair and gently forced her into it. Before he had reached the door she had sprung up again.

'You must search for them! Find everyone you can! Every servant must be taken to scour the roads and hedgerows. That phaeton didn't look safe. I didn't want to let Sylvie ride in it.'

Edgar returned to his wife as she whirled feverishly about the room with a hand gesturing here and a foot stamping there. 'There might be nothing so calamitous to it all, Gloria. The rig might simply have lost a bolt or one of the nags might have thrown a shoe…'

The door bursting open at that point curtailed Edgar's desperate mitigation for June's failure to bring home her younger sister. He rushed towards the man striding into the parlour.

'Is there any news?'

The exact phrase that Edgar had been about to utter was in fact barked at him by his son-in-law. As Edgar shook his head, William swiped a hand across the bluish bristle on his chin. 'I have spoken to Etienne and Isabel,' he concisely informed them as he paced back and forth like a caged animal. 'They have not seen June and Sylvie today. But Isabel recounted something that I did not know. Gavin Blackmore has told June he has a sister in the Fleet. June has been charged to keep the information confidential for Gavin did not want pity or charity. Nevertheless he has allowed June to donate money and clothes to take to his sister to help her.'

'Is that significant at all, do you think?' A glimmer of hope elevated Edgar's heavy brows. 'Would

June have asked to visit her? Have they been silly enough to go there?'

'June would never take Sylvie to such an establishment, no matter how charitably inclined she was feeling towards Blackmore's sister.' William's defence of his wife emerged through lips that were white and bracketed with strain. 'But I'm hopeful they have gone somewhere on impulse and are unavoidably delayed by the rainstorm. One of the horses might have thrown a shoe on a slippery road…'

'You see, my dear, William is of the same opinion. We must not think the worst.' A faltering smile accompanied Edgar's reassurance.

'But you must search!' Gloria wailed. 'You must take everyone and search for them in case they are injured or lost. If Mr Blackmore is hurt and cannot protect them, they might be set upon by thieves or…'

'It is dusk. By the time we assemble it will be full dark,' Edgar soothed.

'Get flares…and lanterns!' Gloria screeched.

'Do not upset yourself so, ma'am.' William's tone was kindly heartening, despite the fact his mother-in-law had voiced the same perilous thoughts that were running amok in his own mind. William knew his father-in-law also was gravely worried, for his brave face was becoming florid with tension and his old eyes were suspiciously moist. 'I have already arranged with Herbert that footmen scour the immediate environs of Hyde Park,' William told them both. 'They will be out in full force now, looking for any sign of an abandoned vehicle. Everything will be done that can be done…'

His determined promise tailed off into a quiet that seemed thick with unspoken fears. 'If they were intending to simply take Sylvie for a ride about the park before returning, then there is only one route of travel to cover. I will join the search party once I have exhausted all other enquiries with family and friends.'

'They would not stay out visiting without sending word!' Gloria insisted. 'June would not worry me so.'

'I know,' William said simply. 'But they might be marooned and unable to get a message to us.' William knew the excuse was feeble. But every fibre of his being resisted pondering the unthinkable: his wife and sister-in-law might be lying dead or injured in an overturned high-flyer. 'I have come directly here from quizzing my parents. June didn't mention to them where she and Blackmore might go next. Do you recall seeing any other people they might have talked to in Hyde Park?'

'As I was leaving them Lord Malvern came by.

I expect, as he is a friend of yours, he would have passed the time of day with them. Lady Forsythe was out with him in his curricle.' The words tripped over each other as Gloria frantically imparted any snippet that might be of help in finding her daughters.

'I shall speak to Adam at once,' William said. He then addressed Edgar. 'Etienne has said he will go and check whether Rachel and Connor have seen them. Will you go and see any other friends and relatives you can think of who may have tempted them away somewhere?'

Upon Edgar's nod, William immediately took his leave of his parents'-in-law and was soon striding from the house.

'Missing?' The single word was expelled in disbelief.

'You and Lady Forsythe were possibly the last people to speak to June before she and Sylvie set off with Blackmore. Did June give any hint where they might go next?'

Adam Townsend shook his head. 'I barely had an opportunity to talk to your wife. Lady Forsythe was conversing with her while I fielded Mrs Prothero's invitation to her chit's ball on Saturday. I saw Blackmore demonstrating how to handle the ribbons to your sister-in-law, then it started to rain…'

He shot an aghast frown at William. 'My God! You don't think he would have let her drive in that perilous weather, do you? They might have had an accident.'

William's face slumped into his hands and he gritted out, 'Do not say that! They are simply delayed. One of his infernal horses might have taken lame.'

Adam came around his desk and gripped William's shoulder. 'You are right, of course,' he encouraged quietly. 'They are probably sheltering somewhere. We'll search until we find them.'

'I have a search party out. They are concentrating their efforts about the park. Do you know where Blackmore has been lodging? I asked him once and got no more information from him than he'd taken rooms close to Greyfriars. Stupidly I didn't persevere. I imagined he was reluctant to be specific because he was embarrassed that he couldn't afford decent accommodation.'

'He was always reticent about his circumstances. Personally I didn't bother to ask where he lived. In any case, I doubt they will be there.'

'Every possibility must be investigated!' Immediately William dragged fingers through his hair and a shrug and a sigh were offered in apology for his raised voice.

Adam twitched a smile at him. 'We *will* find them very soon.'

William nodded, yearning for such arrogant confidence to be his. To keep at bay the tormenting demons that sneaked terrifying images into his mind he concentrated on facts. 'Blackmore was forthcoming about his personal life with June, but made her promise not to repeat what he confided…even to me. June unintentionally let slip to Isabel Hauke that Blackmore's sister Bethany had been hounded into the Fleet for her debts. June has been giving him money to take to her.'

'Stranger and stranger…' Adam murmured. 'I had no idea he had a sister. He never spoke of siblings; I assumed he was an only child.'

'As you say,' William said, 'he was secretive about his circumstances.'

'Why would he choose your wife…a woman he barely knows…as a confidante? You say June has given him cash and been charged not to tell you about it?'

William and Adam exchanged a long look. 'What are you thinking?' Adam finally asked in a voice that was rather hoarse.

'The same as you, I expect,' William said with a hint of anger overcoming his anxiety. 'I'm thinking that perhaps there is something queer in all this.'

'I know he has a way of inveigling that is admirably successful. Percy Carstairs was gulled just before we quit Eton. He gave over fifty guineas to Blackmore for contraband. The geneva and cognac were, according to Blackmore, not forthcoming because The Revenue had confiscated the lot. Carstairs was too credulous to challenge him over it. My investigation turned up that Blackmore had sold the entire stock elsewhere and kept all the profit.'

For the first time in many hours a ghost of a smile curved William's strained lips. 'I would not have had Blackmore for such an enterprising fellow.'

'Neither would I. I had to admit to admiring his audacity. But Percy Carstairs was a friend. We kept it quiet for Percy felt a numbskull to have been so easily duped.'

'We? Why were you involved in it?'

'I felt compelled to help,' Adam drily explained. 'After all, the fifty guineas were mine. Carstairs borrowed the money.'

'I recall you gave Blackmore a hiding. No one seemed to know why and Blackmore just acted the martyr over it.'

'If he has put your wife and Silver in jeopardy in some sordid scheme, I'll make sure he really suffers this time.'

'Not before I do,' William countered with deadly

softness. So deep were William's troubled thoughts now that it didn't occur to him to enquire how his friend knew young Sylvie's true name was Silver.

'I shall go to Lady Forsythe's and find out if she has any light to shed on matters. Your wife might have told her something relevant about their plans for the afternoon.'

William nodded his gratitude. 'And there's only one way to know if Bethany Blackmore has benefited from June's benevolence: go to the Fleet prison and ask her.'

Chapter Sixteen

'**O**pen this door at once!' June's shouting and hammering were to no avail, her efforts mocked by branches strumming on the window and wind piping in the chimney. The mournful concert made June spin about and watch an eerily quivering curtain. Then once again the locked door had her full attention. She banged repeatedly on the paint-peeling panels until her wrists ached.

'Where are we? Has that fiend gone and left us all alone?'

'Thank Heavens you have woken up!' June sped back to the bed and, leaning over her shivering sister, put a hand to Sylvie's clammy brow. 'How do you feel?'

'I'm cold and my head aches,' Sylvie grumbled, but none the less she struggled upright, still snuggled into the bed quilt.

June cupped one of her sister's icy cheeks and, by the light of the small stump of candle Blackmore had stuck on a shaky shelf, carefully scrutinised her appearance.

'Do I look a mess?' Sylvie asked in a tone that was curious rather than anxious.

'Your hair is like a bird's nest and you have a bruise on your jaw.' June combed back the platinum tangles and touched the purple blotch with fingers that were infinitely gentle. Quickly she took off her cloak and used it as an extra cover for Sylvie.

'Where are we? Are we prisoners?'

'Hostages, to be more accurate,' June told her. 'Blackmore let on, when he was carrying you up the stairs to this room, that we shall be held until a ransom is paid.'

Sylvie attempted to smile, but winced as it caused her injury to twinge. 'Is it still raining? Shall we jump from the window and get away?' she rattled off. 'I suppose I ought try to escape and save Papa the expense. He is already moaning about the cost of my come-out. Of course, that *is* a waste of money.'

'Papa would give everything he has to keep you safe and never begrudge a penny piece.' June went to the casement, rubbing briskly at her arms to ward off the chill air. She peered into dismal blackness whilst trying to fathom where on earth they might be.

During their hectic flight out of London, dying light and drizzle had blurred woods, fields, villages into a bolt of brown until June, hampered further by tears, no longer had any idea in which direction, or how far, they had travelled. It had been dusk, with wind coursing the rain clouds to the horizon, when Gavin Blackmore finally turned the phaeton off the road and on to a sludgy track. June had watched a ghostly outline solidify into a lime-washed lodge as they moved closer over the ruts.

With his arms occupied carrying Sylvie's coma-tose form, their captor had aimed urgent kicks at the door until an oafish-looking man had let them in. Blackmore had addressed the fellow as Cursley with an abruptness that denoted him as a menial.

There had been little time to look about the interior for Gavin had ushered her straight to the stairs, forcing her to mount them and enter this spartanly furnished chamber. June judged they had probably arrived less than an hour ago, yet the minutes seemed to have dragged interminably until she felt sure she had counted each stitch in the bed quilt and every nail in the door that barred their freedom.

Now she focussed on an impenetrable dark beyond the window. She could just detect the outline of the phaeton and horses still tethered to it. If only they could reach that vehicle and have a few minutes' head start, she would soon grasp the knack of steering the contraption. She sighed on realising how futile was any hope of escape. If they managed to hoodwink Blackmore, there was still the gigantic Cursley to dodge.

But for a taper in a window below pitching yellow on to the ground, and an occasional murmur of voices, they might have been alone in the house. June let the curtain fall back into place. 'We certainly cannot escape through this small opening. Besides, I am not sure where we are and it is so dark now we might wander into a bog or ditch or get set upon by thieves.'

She returned to the bed to sit beside Sylvie and chafed her freezing hands between her palms. 'Daylight and providence will be needed to get us away from Blackmore and his toady.' At Sylvie's enquiring look she explained. 'It seems our abductor has an accomplice. But no sign of Bethany, whom he promises we shall meet!' June suddenly hugged Sylvie to her. 'I'm so sorry to have got you embroiled in all this. If only I hadn't been so foolish as to have been taken in by Blackmore's cock-and-bull story.'

The purpling mark on Sylvie's jaw made her look poignantly vulnerable and only served to heighten June's feelings of guilt. 'But we shall not try to escape unless there is a good chance we might get clean away in the phaeton. We must be sensible. If we risk fleeing on foot, we might be prey to thieves or the elements.'

'There are worse hazards in you attempting to drive that rig.'

It was cheekily said, but June noticed that some of her sister's buoyancy was flagging. Sylvie was wrapping herself into her blanket, her eyes huge and luminous in the candlelit dusk. June stroked her face encouragingly. 'If we do not get an opportunity to bolt, you must be my brave girl until William comes for us and takes us home.'

'How will William know where we are?'

June made to utter some empty reassurance, but she swallowed the platitude. Her sister might be young, but she was no fool and June would not treat her as such. 'They will even now be searching for us. We must hope that Papa and William and our brothers-in-law make investigations and find out Blackmore is a villain and which places he frequents. I'm sure eventually they *will* trace us to this house.'

'It is not your fault that I am here.' Sylvie smiled kindly on sensing June's self-torment. 'I could have gone straight home with Mama, but I didn't want to. I know you were being nice by letting me ride with you. I wouldn't have minded if you had escaped on the road and left me behind, for you could have raised the alarm.' A whimsical look misted Sylvie's eyes. 'I'm not frightened, anyhow. Lord Malvern is coming to rescue me. Before I woke up just now I dreamed he would.'

'Well, I hope you are right,' June said.

'So do I,' mocked a voice from the door. Gavin Blackmore sauntered into the room...but not too far. He stood close enough to the exit to prevent June slipping through it. 'How marvellous it would be if Townsend came here begging me on his knees to spare you. Unfortunately, I doubt an innocent maid would tempt that reprobate into acting the hero. You're pretty enough, but Townsend likes his women seasoned. Of course, if your father fails to meet my demands, I will personally ensure that before you leave here you have all the experience you need to keep his lordship besotted for a year or more.'

June stepped in front of Sylvie so she was screened from view. 'What demands? What have you done? Have you sent word to William where we are? He will kill you for this outrage.'

'If he is foolish enough to defy me, your family will never see either of you again. My man Cursley is on an errand to deliver letters to William and your father. I'm sure your husband will act the loving spouse and give me what I want to recover what he wants.'

'And what is it you want?' June demanded angrily.

'I want you. But, against my will and my instinct, I haven't told your husband that. I know you still love William, despite the rumours of adultery and my efforts to turn you against him. So I'll act the martyr and instead settle for five thousand of his pounds.' Blackmore mentioned the sum impenitently.

June echoed the amount in astonishment.

'Indeed. It should get me to the Americas before the duns find me again.'

'So it was *you* who had run up debts, not the fictitious Bethany Blackmore?'

Gavin adopted a hurt look. 'Why do you persist in thinking she is a figment of my imagination? Be patient a while longer and you will meet Bethany in the flesh, I promise.' He strolled closer to the sisters. His finger managed to idly brush the bruise he had given Sylvie before she recoiled and smacked away his hand.

'But you are right,' Gavin said, unperturbed by Sylvie's disgust as he stationed himself close to the door again. 'I have been hounded by those curs, Bethany, too, and she *was* in the Fleet for her misdemeanours. You cannot accuse me of telling *only* lies, Mrs Pemberton, for I have simply tailored falsehood with truth to fit my needs.'

'I cannot believe that once I regarded you as a friend,' June flung at him contemptuously. 'What a fool I have been!'

'Don't rue your kindness,' he said with an unexpected sincerity. 'I'm grateful to you, and so is Bethany, for she did receive the fine clothes you donated.' His interest again became intimate. 'William is a very lucky man to have such an alluring wife. If I did not hold you in such high regard, I might be tempted to…' A low-lidded gaze lingered lustfully on her.

Suddenly he laughed. 'Enough! Of course we are friends and as such I respect you too much to take advantage of your position as my prisoner. I hope your family do not force me to act the brute with either of you.' Another smouldering look was slanted at June. 'It is fair the tables are turned, for you captivated me from the start. With a little more manipulation I'm confident you would have agreed to us becoming lovers. Then, of course, there would have been no more need for subterfuge. As my mistress you would have willingly paid my debts. Perhaps you would have come to America with me…'

June darted a quizzical look at him. 'You are obviously deluded to think so.' Suddenly her amazement transformed to suspicion. *A little more* *manipulation…turn you against him…*were phrases filtering back into her mind. 'In the ridiculous belief that you might bring about such a fantasy, did you instigate some of the scandal that was circulating simply to drive us apart?'

Gavin chuckled. 'Lord Harley and his friend had already succeeded in causing discord between you and William. I was unaware of their intention to make mischief, but gratefully exploited it. I hoped you would be suspicious and hurt and would eventually turn to me for solace. But you seemed determined to love your husband no matter what scandals were bandied about. Of course, I had heard talk that you wanted children. I thought that, if you believed William had already sired a child with another, it might be the final straw and kill your devotion to him. I confess I sowed that seed. I'll admit that Bethany sought to benefit from it, too. She can be a greedy minx when she scents money, rash and incautious too. We argued over that.'

'What do you mean…over that?' June demanded.

'She was too impatient and sent William a blackmail note. It was a silly attempt to make a quick profit, for there was no longer a secret to keep from you. The rumour I started was already in circulation, I made sure of that.' He gestured in emphasis. 'Besides, had Bethany known William as I do, she

would have realised it was a wasted effort. He
might be a quiet man, but your husband is too
strong a character to bow to blackmail.'

Blackmore sighed his disappointment. 'It is a
shame things have gone awry. I'm sure I would
have won you over eventually. You are quite right
for me, generous and sweet. And I know you understand my torments...how envy can burrow deep
within a person and rot their soul. We are kindred
spirits, you and I.'

'We are nothing of the sort! Don't you dare say
otherwise.' June gulped a breath, attempting to sti-
fle her anger, for she knew there was a grain of
truth in his ramblings. He had recognised in her
disposition flaws that made her ashamed, flaws that
had made her compassionate and blind to a swin-
dler's true nature.

She also understood quite clearly the threats lurk-
ing in his compliments. He was desperate for cash;
should the ransom demand not be met swiftly
enough, he would, without compunction, act the
abuser out of revenge. If he attempted to perpetrate
such horror, she would fight him tooth and nail and
she knew Sylvie would too. The thought of Sylvie
defiled and beaten made her blood alternately boil,
then flow cold. 'You are insane, not disadvantaged,'
she hissed. 'The only way you could prove otherwise would be to set us both free immediately. If

you do that, you also will have time to abscond before the authorities catch up with you. Kidnap and extortion carry high penalties. I promise to speak in your defence and will say you treated us well.'

'Bravo! A fine attempt, but, alas, it will not work.' He smiled ruefully. 'I am not sure how Bethany endured being incarcerated. I would rather kill myself than go to such a hell-hole. That is why I have striven to keep the duns at bay through your generosity, but they will be back.' He tilted his head to assess her. 'You are becoming quite…bold and confident. I am not sure I like that, June. I shall call you June now, for there is a special bond of intimacy between us, you cannot deny it. I must say that I'm also disappointed you no longer seem as keen as once you were to meet Bethany. Ah…' He cocked his head, excitement glittering in his mild brown eyes. 'How timely! I expect that is her now. I suppose she will have brought with her that tiresome…'

June missed the rest of his speech, for she too had heard a vehicle outside. She rushed to the window and, lifting the curtain, squinted out. Through wind-tossed branches she saw that a carriage had stopped by the door. A woman in a hooded cloak stepped down into a lantern-lit pool of light, then a diminutive figure, similarly swaddled against the elements, followed. The carriage immediately pulled away again. The key scraping in the lock curtailed June's curious peering at the intriguing silhouettes. She flew from the window to the door and yanked at the handle, shouting, 'Come back, you beast, and let us out!'

'I have discovered something very odd.'

'So have I,' was Adam's concise response to William's unceremonious greeting.

The two men had just arrived back, with timely precision, at William's elegant townhouse. In unison they took the front steps two at a time.

Once inside William's walnut-panelled study, Adam strode to the fire and held out his palms to the blaze. 'Did you find this Bethany woman at the Fleet?'

'I did not, but a couple of sovereigns soon oiled the tongue of a gregarious cove by the name of Tommy Barr, who was happy to tell me all he knew about her. He confirmed Bethany Blackmore was recently detained there. Her debts came about when she rented flamboyant premises in Mayfair for her business as a bawd, then absconded without paying the landlord. She tried to intimidate him and the other turnkeys into giving her privileges by threatening them with dire consequences should they not be forthcoming. When that didn't work, she resorted to payment in kind for favours.'

Adam grunted a laugh. 'If she *is* a relation of Blackmore's, it's little wonder that he keeps his home life private.'

'Those were my thoughts. I asked about her visitors. A gentleman fitting Blackmore's description brought her some clothing, for her own had been torn when she was attacked by another bawd who thought she was acting above her station.'

Adam stuck his warmed hands in his pockets. He arrowed a slanting glance at William's haggard features. 'It's welcome news. The more intrigue we uncover, the less likely it is that the phaeton has come to grief in the storm.'

William nodded, his eyes wide and desperate. 'Bethany fed her gaolers some salacious titbits about her influential clients when attempting to wheedle favours. She stopped short of naming names, but bragged about a secluded hunting lodge in Finsbury Park where a talented courtesan—a friend of hers and a society lady—discreetly entertains Quality. I know of White Lodge in the vicinity. Some years ago now I went there on a shooting party. It belongs to the Carlisle estate.'

'Robbie Carlisle had a reputation as a whoremonger. Is the decrepit old fool dead yet?' Adam asked.

William shrugged. 'I haven't seen him in a while.' Recalling Adam had some news to impart, he asked, 'What did you learn from Lady Forsythe?'

'In light of what you have just told me, I have discovered something very peculiar. Lady Forsythe's sister once lived in Devon quite close to the Blackmore family. By all accounts there were only two children born to the Reverend and Mrs Blackmore. The mother died when the daughter was born and the daughter died of illness when she was a youngster. Lady Forsythe said that she and June were talking about that just this afternoon.'

'June would not have hesitated in challenging Blackmore if she thought he had been intentionally duping her.' William stared at his friend, his face ashen with anxiety. 'I can't think straight any more. Would he resort to violence or crime to keep safe his secrets?'

Herbert's appearance on the threshold prevented Adam from giving his opinion on Blackmore's capacity for evil. 'There is a gentleman here to see you, sir.' The butler stood aside to reveal a figure dressed in a dun-brown travelling cape standing just behind him in the hallway.

Before Herbert could return to his duties, William asked urgently, 'Is there any news from the search party?'

'No, sir,' Herbert said. 'I'm sorry...' he added softly before his slight, dark figure melted into the shadows.

The newcomer immediately doffed his hat and stuck it beneath an arm. 'H'I'm sorry to call late, sir, but h'I have taken it upon myself to suppose rightly or wrongly that what h'I have uncovered in the county of Devon—from which h'I am just re-turned—appertaining to the background of a certain lady and her child might be so important to you as to make you angry should you wait till tomorrow when in fact h'I could have brought you the news sooner, for it might be—'

'For pity's sake, tell me what it is you know, man!' William bawled with uncustomary churlish-ness. 'And be quick about it, for there is much work to do.'

The detective flicked a glance between the two gentlemen and sucked his teeth before saying in a deeply cautioning tone, 'H'it's news of a sensitive, shocking nature...'

'Be assured we are braced and ready,' William said with a sigh.

Chapter Seventeen

'*This* is Bethany?' June's voice, when she finally found it, emerged in a breathless squeak.

So much that was preposterous had occurred recently that June felt sure she was inured to the bizarre. But the sight greeting her, as Gavin ushered them into a snug parlour, rendered her transfixed.

'Of course it is not,' Blackmore mockingly chided. 'It is Lady Bingham…or Celeste as she calls herself professionally. You cannot have forgotten her; I know you visited her just this afternoon. I learned that from the letter I received, for it was her work, not Bethany's.' In an under-breath he muttered, 'I apologise for her presence. I have little liking for the bitch either.' Turning, he beckoned to someone else. '*This* is Bethany.'

June had overlooked the slight cloaked figure as that of a child. But as a woman's head emerged from the confines of an enveloping hood, a pair of dark cynical eyes challenged her. 'It is unlikely she is your *younger* sister.' June was no longer interested in knowing how Bethany was related to Gavin. In a daze, she was attempting to comprehend how a gentlewoman—even one as indecorous as Lady Bingham—might be in cahoots with the Blackmores. Her memory dredged up a single fact that might link them—they hailed from the same part of the West Country.

'Bethany is my stepmother and *very* wicked,' Blackmore introduced the woman with a grin. 'My father rued the day he married her, for then she was no longer the God-fearing Christian she had seemed while keen to remain employed as his housekeeper.' A sly look that made June's skin creep passed between the two. 'We have always got on famously for the most part.' Blackmore sauntered away to the inglenook and poked at a small grate until orange lights sparked amid the embers.

While his back was turned June urgently addressed Lady Bingham. 'I have no idea why you are here, but I'm sure you cannot know that we have been kidnapped and threatened with violence. You must help us. Make him see sense and set us free immediately.'

Constance's only reaction was to narrow her eyes in consideration.

'Why do you hesitate?' June demanded. 'Do you want to be thought a party to such an evil crime?' She watched Constance slide a look of furious despising at Gavin. Desperately she repeated, 'Why do you hesitate? You must know your reputation will be tainted by your association with this madman.'

'I do know that very well!' Constance finally responded in a voice made husky with contempt. 'You lily-livered blockhead! You have panicked and ruined everything.'

'*I* have ruined everything?' he sneered. 'If you could control that infernal itch between your legs, we would still be cosy in Devon and with cash in our pockets.'

'But for me you'd still be working dawn till dusk in a musty clerk's office for a pittance! The cash you had in your pocket was put there by my efforts! And you repay me with stupidity!'

'It is not all Gavin's fault! Mind your tongue or you will have me to answer to!' Bethany barked in a rough voice that belied her tiny stature. With her hands planted on her hips she studied the assembled company whilst pacing back and forth.

June assessed Gavin's stepmother with a female eye. So this virago was Bethany, the delicate soul on whom she had squandered her compassion and charity. She might have been about forty-five years old, yet she had the wiry slenderness of a much younger woman. There was silver shining in her dark coarse hair and some crinkles about her eyes that betrayed her age, but she was certainly handsome if extraordinarily petite.

'You cannot deny he has acted stupidly,' Constance reasoned, illustrating her exasperation with a flick of a hand. 'Since he started that absurd rumour about William Pemberton siring Cissy it is all gone awry. William has sent detectives to Devon to investigate. I made it plain in my letter we must proceed with caution. Caution! Hah! Just look what he has done!'

'You were not above conniving when you thought it would get you Pemberton's protection,' Gavin sniped. 'You could have quashed the gossip. You have only decided to despise the idea since he rejected you out of hand.'

Constance glared at him, with indignant colour bright as rouge on a marionette spotting her cheeks. 'I can have any man I want…when I want,' she hissed.

'I beg to differ, my dear,' Gavin drawled. 'Pemberton and myself are just two gentlemen I know who are disinclined to dally with a tawdry jade.'

'That is just *one* gentleman and a eunuch who would be fortunate to ever again get such a chance,' returned the lady with acid sweetness. She smiled with vicious triumph as her insult blanched Gavin's complexion.

Constance intercepted the brooding look he shot at June. 'Has he threatened to violate you? You have little to fear...' An elegant white hand raised and a small finger wiggled in lewd belittlement.

'You bitch, I'll kill you!' Blackmore suddenly lunged across the room at her but was prevented from lashing out as Bethany sprang between them.

'Enough of this!' The roaring baritone would not have disgraced a navvy. 'You are *both* imbeciles!' Bethany sent threatening stares between them, pacing backwards. She turned her shrewd eyes on the blonde sisters.

Instinctively June had cradled Sylvie against her side as though to protect her from the violence in the room. Now the combatants had quietened, yet so keenly did June sense an air of menace that she pushed Sylvie behind her back.

Bethany Blackmore crept around their fused forms as though playing a game, but all the while she was seriously intent on investigating the adolescent beauty in June's shadow. Suddenly she took a tress of platinum hair, stroked it across her palm while testing its silken weight.

Sylvie snatched herself free of the woman's impertinent touch and in doing so fully exposed her face and figure.

'Gavin's got us treasure all right! Spirit as well as looks!' Bethany chuckled contentedly. 'Waiting for ransom money will take too long and bring the dragoons as well as their kin down on our heads.' She looked slyly at her stepson. 'Save your lechery for the elder, the younger is out of bounds. There are several gentlemen who would gladly pay a king's ransom to feast a while on such pure honey. But we have no time for an auction. There is one close by, and I know he would willingly pay tonight, whatever I ask, to be first.' Her rising excitement was evident in the glitter in her sly eyes. 'By this time tomorrow we could all be at Newhaven. Then, once safe in France, we can arrange passage to the Americas.'

Listening to their foul plan to barter Sylvie's virginity made June tense with wrath. William would be searching for them, she was sure, but equally she realised it would now be a miracle should he find them before Sylvie was sold to a disgusting debauchee.

Waiting for a good chance to escape now seemed absurd rather than sensible. Getting Sylvie immediately away from these vile people was imperative. But to do so they must employ some daring and cunning of their own. Quickly she pivoted about and, before hugging Sylvie, strove to convey her wordless instructions to her sister with her eyes.

'You have made my sister ill! Can't you see she is about to be sick after listening to your diabolical scheme?'

Sylvie's acute mind immediately comprehended her role. Her arms crossed her middle as though she had a cramp and she bent forward with ballooning cheeks.

Constance Bingham looked askance at Sylvie's bobbing throat. 'For God's sake, quickly, get the girl some hartshorn. I hardly think Lord Carlisle will relish taking his pleasure of a chit who stinks of vomit.'

'I must take her upstairs to rest. If she becomes hysterical she might have one of her seizures.'

'Seizures?' Blackmore echoed.

'She is prone to fits brought on by extreme fear or excitement.'

'Indeed?' Bethany Blackmore's smirk said she guessed the indisposition was dubious. 'Luckily I have a cure. A dose of my laudanum will calm her well enough for Carlisle to have his fun.'

'I must take her upstairs!' June shrieked and imperceptibly nudged at Sylvie's ribs for her to intensify the drama. Sylvie obliged by groaning and clamping her hands over her mouth.

'For God's sake, take her away before she *is* sick!' Lady Bingham cried, with a look of sheer distaste creasing her features.

A flick of Bethany's head at the door was enough permission for June to steer her sister towards it. A backward glare at Blackmore as they mounted the stairs showed that he was observing them from where he had astutely stationed himself in the hallway.

Once the chamber door was shut, June whispered urgently, 'We must escape, but not in the phaeton, for Blackmore is suspicious and will be upon us before we are able to move it a yard. You must be my brave girl, Sylvie, and get away first. Run for your life once you are outside. I will follow shortly and find you. Secrete yourself somewhere till daylight and I promise I *will* come and find you. Put on my cloak.'

Sylvie did as she was bid, but her large blue eyes were wide and fearful. 'How will we escape? That monster is downstairs guarding the door.'

'I know, but there must be a way!' June sent searching glances about the chamber, desperately looking for something, anything, that might serve as a weapon. The empty china pitcher, should she smash it, might provide sharp shards, but how would they overcome three adversaries? A diversion was needed… By the light of the candle-stump she peered out of the window as though for some inspiration. A draught flicked an edge of flimsy curtain towards the flame and instinctively June cupped a hand about the wick. A glimmer of an idea came to mind.

'It would be a perilous risk…' Sylvie ventured, a natural acuity having alerted her to June's thoughts.

'Yes, but there is a perilous risk if you stay here,' June uttered softly. She said no more, for she did not want to panic Sylvie with examples of depravity. Her mouth had dried with terror at the thought of her sweet sister's fate should either Blackmore or Lord Carlisle get their hands on her. Forcefully she said, 'It is the only way, Sylvie! You must be ready to flee. Never fear that you will be hunted down. They are three cowards who will only be interested in saving their own miserable skins once they know the house is afire.'

Sylvie nodded, unblinking, as she drew courage from June's confidence.

Quickly June tore a strip of linen from her petticoat and held it to the candle. As soon as it was alight she made a nest in the quilt, coddling the flame with her breath until it smouldered and opened a circular hole from which down drifted like snow. As the fire took hold, June quickly embraced Sylvie, then determinedly put her from her. In a fluid movement she smashed the pitcher against the bedstead, muffling the sound with the blankets. She gave Sylvie the sharpest shard she could find and took one herself.

'I don't want to go without you,' Sylvie uttered on a sob.

June put a hand over her sister's quivering mouth. 'I shall be soon with you, I promise. You must run and run and never look back. When it is daylight I *will* find you.'

Sylvie nodded.

With a deep breath and a glance at the flames dancing on the bed, June flung open the door. 'Quick! Come at once!' she called in a husky hiss so Blackmore alone would be summoned. Sylvie might slip past one of their enemies; she would not evade three.

When their guard did little more than glance quizzically up at her, June sped to the top of the stairs. 'You fool! There is a fire! The candle is over-set!'

June's silhouette suddenly acquired an amber aura. After a second of stupefaction, during which his reaction was limited to an open-mouthed goggle, Blackmore pounded up the stairs whilst spitting out a string of oaths. Once he was in the room, the sight that confronted him had him baring his teeth in frustration. He rushed to the washstand where once the water jug had rested.

'Go!' June propelled her sister through the door. 'I will not let him come after you, I promise.'

Sylvie opened her mouth to protest, but her sister's fierce look and rough push had her fleeing silently down the stairs, through the door and into the night.

'What in damnation is that?'

The two riders reined in. Adam pointed off to the distance. 'Over there!'

'It looks like a fire,' William said, peering at a nebulous yellow light arcing into the night sky. He turned in the saddle. Through the dusk his eyes gleamed wide and alert at Adam. 'We must be close now. It could be a signal. Please God, if that is White Lodge and they are there, don't let it be anything other than a signal.' He kneed his horse forward and was soon thundering towards the burning building with Adam close behind.

'And what the hell was that?' Adam reined in so hard his stallion pranced and pawed at air. A shadowy cloaked figure started, then darted into the trees close by.

'Show yourself!' William roared, taking his horse in a wide circle and thundering back towards the fringe of woodland that had swallowed up the fugitive. 'Who is there?' he bellowed again as he peered through barring trunks.

'William?' a croaky voice called.

'Is that you, Sylvie?' William had dismounted in an instant.

Sylvie was soon running forward, her sobbing gasps shaking her body as she launched herself at her brother-in-law's chest. 'June is still Blackmore's prisoner and she said I must keep running and she will follow me and find me...but I'm frightened...I don't want her to die in the fire.'

'June won't die!' The vow was forcefully expelled in a tone so raw each word tore at William's throat. In seconds he was racing back to his horse. 'Keep her safe!' was slung back over his shoulder at Adam.

Adam encircled Sylvie's body lightly with an arm. She immediately plucked away the restraint. 'I must go back and help. I could not bear it if June should perish. I wanted her to come with me, but she made me go first...to make sure I got away.' Sylvie's soft bosom heaved in breathlessness against a barring forearm.

'Hush, William will get her.' Adam soothed and once more urged her back against his muscular torso. Gently he smoothed her moonlight hair. 'You must calm yourself. Your sister will be angry if you again put yourself in jeopardy when she has risked all for you. Your other brothers-in-law are bringing the dragoons. They are close behind us.'

Adam's wise words had little effect on Sylvie, who fiercely pushed and pulled in vain at his arm. Finally she pivoted about, kicking at him until she broke free. She had sprinted a yard or two when Adam caught her and, with an oath beneath his breath, swung her into his arms to protect his shins from further assault. When repeated reassurance and reason were to no avail, and his face became a new target, he hoisted her over his shoulder and strode back to his horse.

Having transferred the spitfire to his stallion, he swung into the saddle before sitting her upright. He deftly dodged the proof that her hysteria was unabated and set off after William in the direction of the blazing Lodge.

'For pity's sake! There is still time for us to escape the flames!'

'I prefer death to capture, I told you that.'

'Well, I beg you will let *me* go.' June's voice was gruff with smoke and pleading.

Blackmore shook his head. 'I told you I wanted you or your husband's money. It is only fair I should get one or the other. Why should William have all? Do you believe in an afterlife, June? I do and should like you there with me. But might you go to Heaven and me to Hell, I wonder?'

June squinted through the turgid atmosphere at

her executioner. Blackmore was standing with his back against the door, barring her escape to cool sweet air.

Constance and Bethany had already given up their efforts to persuade their cohort to flee with them in the phaeton. Gavin's stepmother had been the first to lose courage and bolt. Constance had hesitated a moment longer, endorsing June's frantic appeal that Gavin act rationally now the game was up. But the noise of charred timbers splintering had soon startled into flight Lady Bingham's humanity and her person.

June had listened, despairingly, as the carriage rattled away, bearing the women to safety. Now she was left alone, at the mercy of their crazed accomplice.

A burning beam crashed down on to the landing, sending sparks raining into the hallway.

'The thatch is burning! For pity's sake! The roof will collapse.' June's mouth was arid from terror and black motes that were suspended in the thick air. She felt her lungs ache and cupped her hands over her nose to try and filter each breath. *William, I love you…please know I love you…* chanted in her feverish mind as she watched flaming petals curving about the banisters in an inexorable descent towards her.

She pricked her finger with the shard of china in

her pocket. Again and again she tested its sharp edge. But first she needed to get within striking range of him…

June took a step away from the searing heat at her back while conversing as calmly as she was able. 'Did you father Lady Bingham's daughter?'

'I thank God I did not. I would hate a daughter of mine to be reared by a whore.' Blackmore coughed as the heat and smoke attacked his throat. 'Now you think me a hypocrite, for I expect you have guessed that Bethany and Constance are alike. Both have catered to the basic needs of men. But Bethany is a businesswoman; Constance simply worships the work. We had a sweet trade in Devon, but she put it all in jeopardy with her insatiable appetite. We had fine gentlemen clients who paid well. They didn't take kindly to discovering that *Celeste* was dallying with the dregs of humanity. Quality make bad enemies. Even her daughter's father could not prevent her from acting like a bitch in heat… Enough!' he suddenly shouted. 'Enough of her and fornication! I should like *us* to be lovers before we die. I should like one last earthly pleasure.'

June stepped closer to him, feeling the heat of burning detritus beneath her shoes.

'If I kiss you would that be enough to save us both?' she said huskily.

He grinned, a strip of white in his soot-stained face. 'As we are friends I must be honest and say I doubt it, but it is a start, so please try to persuade me to be kind.' He held out his arms in mocking invitation.

June wondered whether her complexion was as grimy as was his. She touched her cheek and felt grit on her fingertips. Her face angled to his at the same moment one of her hands began withdrawing the weapon from her pocket.

A violent battering at the door put a split in the planks and a palsy in Blackmore's limbs.

He recovered quickly and sprang sideways. 'Pemberton, the conquering hero…' Gavin sneered, his teeth bared in frustration. 'What a shame! For me he is too early and for you he is too late.' He fastened an arm chokingly about June's neck, pulling her backwards and off balance, just as the door caved in and William burst through the aperture.

'I might have known perfect Pemberton would arrive at the eleventh hour to try and ruin things,' Blackmore screamed across the crackle and hiss of the fire as he dragged June up the stairs towards the inferno.

'Let her go,' William bellowed hoarsely as he paced into the stifling hallway. A hand elevated in supplication, formed an impotent fist. 'Let my wife go and you can go too. I'll help you get away.'

'Of course you will,' Gavin mocked. 'Then I shall be arrested at the coast and taken to stand trial. Do you think I would stay alive at any cost? Stupid! That is not my way. What I fear is a living death rotting on a prison hulk or swinging on a gibbet with the crows at my eyes while I still breathe. But perishing cleanly…ah, that is sweet…'

'Listen to me!' William roared as the hand about June's throat tightened, jerking her smoky blonde head back against her captor's shoulder. 'What is it you want? Money? Name your price.'

'Tell him what I want, sweetheart,' Blackmore whispered to June while touching his lips to her grimy cheek. 'Tell him if he comes closer I will warm your icy heart with the flames. Tell him I can make you burn for me.'

June gasped for breath for a violent heat was stealing the little air she could draw into her lungs. A hand fluttered to her pocket to withdraw the sliver of crockery. With all her strength she stabbed it hard against his thigh.

He howled in pain and surprise and loosened his grip to investigate the damage. The makeshift dagger plunged again and again as June squirmed her head beneath his arm. She stumbled and slid down the treads on collapsing legs while half-blinded eyes saw her husband's face as a mask of torment as he sprang forward to catch her.

Then there was a welcome chill for her scorching limbs and the scent of rain-damp earth to soothe her lungs. And she was sure it was Sylvie's tears that wet her face although she felt her body heaving with sobs. And it might have been a dream that brought horsemen close before again they pounded away. But safe in her husband's arms she had only to turn her aching head away to William's chest to rest a while and finally she allowed it.

Chapter Eighteen

'I am not an invalid, you know. I am just tired.'

At those gentle teasing words, William placed down the bowl of broth he had been clumsily pressing on his wife. 'You must eat,' he insisted, while stroking back grimy golden hair to tenderly place his lips on a mucky brow.

'Yes, I know,' June said with a wry smile. 'And I look forward to tucking into a good dinner later.' As she saw her husband's glistening blue eyes roving her face she asked, 'Do I look awful?'

'You look beautiful. You always look beautiful,' he uttered hoarsely and sat down carefully on the edge of the bed.

June removed a hand from beneath the bedcovers where, time and again, he had tucked it in. A soft palm glided over rough stubble on a gaunt cheek. 'Don't cry,' she whispered. 'I am fine…Sylvie is fine…'

William nodded, and taking that delicate dirty hand in his he dipped his forehead to it as though in obeisance. 'Your parents are below, your sisters, too. I have told them you are sleeping, but they will not go away. They want simply to see you. Are you well enough just to say hello?'

'Of course,' June said and pushed herself up on to her elbows. Ten ivory fingers were fanned out and, after a glance to either side of her, she tutted her dismay. 'Heavens! Look at me! The sheets must be black.' She took one of William's hands and turned it over, examining his long, firm fingers. 'Have you not had an opportunity to wash either?'

William glanced at his stained shirt and soiled skin. 'I don't know…I have stayed here with you. It did not occur to me…' He paused before adding, 'Your pretty new clothes are ruined.' He looked towards the chair where he had lobbed those flimsy scraps she had worn for the first time.

On returning to the house close to dawn he had refused to leave her side for a moment. Her maid, Verity, had thus discreetly withdrawn, visibly distressed by her mistress's condition. William had carefully removed the tattered muslin from his wife's limp form until she swayed drowsily against him in only her undergarments. He had put her beneath the pristine covers, then collapsed beside her with his eyes fixed on her still profile.

She had slept for more than ten hours as though dead, without movement, although the physician who had examined her in that time said he could find no damage other than minor blisters and scrapes, and a lock of singed hair. Her bruised mind was of prime concern and had sought its own cure, he had said with a respectful nod to the wisdom of nature. Handing over a pot of unguent, he had advised William not to fret and William had blinked and lied.

'Send them all up. Afterwards I want to bathe—so must you—and then I want to dine.'

William sniffed, swiped moisture from his nose and smiled diffidently.

'And then I want you to love me, William…I want so much that you love me before I sleep again.'

He nodded, his lips tightly compressed, and stood up with an indrawn breath that seemed to take an inordinately long time to fill his lungs. He went to the window, quietly appreciating a glorious spring afternoon until it restored his composure. 'I'll fetch your family,' he finally said.

'For a man who in the early hours of today rode for two-score miles on horseback, kicked down a door and rescued a fair lady, you still have a surprising lot of energy, sir.'

'And it's not spent yet,' William wolfishly warned his wife as he lowered his head to hers and took her swollen scarlet mouth in a deep drugging kiss.

June flexed like a languid kitten beneath him while skimming her hands over the hard ridges of muscle spanning the breadth of his back. She revelled in the taste and scent of him, the sensation of his body moulded to hers.

At first they had made love tenderly, as usual, but when William would have cuddled her protectively against his side in a prelude to sleep she had tantalised his long, lean body with subtle fingertip touches.

'I am alive…and well, William,' she had whispered against his warm musky skin. 'Prove it to me…please…as never before…' The wooing sweetness of his next kiss was welcomed with a nip from her small teeth. Softly sensual caresses tempted her to dig her nails into the muscle bulging in his braced arms.

Alert to his wife's wordless plea, in every sense he had obliged her. Kisses of exquisite savagery had bruised her lips. Her breasts had engorged and ached from the torture of endless attention before rhythmic thrusts had ground at her pelvis, so hard and deep, that she was jerked, moaning, from mattress to wall. Still she imprisoned him with silken limbs coiled at his head and hips and artfully enticed for more vital knowledge of her existence.

Their violent passion had sent the damp bedspread to trail the floor and with a languid hand June now drew it up over William's back so it formed a shelter for their exhausted bodies.

Sated and warm and with her mind sensually drugged she was ready to know…

'Did the dragoons catch up with Constance and Bethany?'

'Yes. They were arrested and will stand trial for aiding and abetting. I expect, when all is laid open to scrutiny, other charges will be laid against them too.'

The unspoken question thickened the atmosphere until June burst out huskily, 'Is Gavin Blackmore dead?'

William eventually answered hoarsely, 'I tried to reach him, so did Adam, but he refused to live and walked into the fire. I wanted to see him swing, or kill him myself, but he got his way and perished cleanly.'

June saw the torment in his eyes. With a kiss transferred from a finger to his lips, she attempted to soothe his pain. 'You were not to know how sick was his mind. I chose to spend time with him and, despite all our troubles and arguments, you kindly did not object. You rarely object to what I want, do you?' she praised him softly. 'I have always deemed myself fortunate to have a husband who so readily bestows on me respect and independence.'

'Kind words won't do, June.' William shook his head. 'You have suffered horribly because of my neglect. I might have lost you,' he uttered, so hoarsely the words were almost inaudible. 'You are the most precious thing to me, yet I allowed you to be escorted and befriended by a man I never really liked and whom I had not seen in a decade. I knew Blackmore at school and even then he was… different.' He caught at June's small hands as they moved to comfort him. 'No! I must declare it or my conscience will rack me my life through.' He paused before adding, 'Adam knew Gavin to be a liar who had attempted to swindle money from a fellow student. Now Townsend feels he must share the blame for keeping that intelligence to himself.'

'If we are all to unburden ourselves of guilt, then I have confessions to make too,' June said quietly. 'I enjoyed receiving Gavin's flattery.' She smiled wryly. 'Of course, I see now that he intended to impress me. But my own behaviour was not impeccable. I guessed that he wanted to be more than the friend I considered him, yet I did not put a stop to our outings. I encouraged his attention from vanity.' She touched William's face with loving fingers. 'And I allowed the gossips to poison my mind.

I began to deem you capable of committing adultery, yet previously you had never given me reason to doubt your loyalty. I was jealous, especially when I saw Constance shamelessly embracing you on her doorstep. I could have challenged you over it, and believed what you told me, but instead I rejected you and went out to meet Gavin.'

William lowered himself to lie beside his wife and took her in his arms. 'The mischief-makers did their work well. It was always their intention to corrupt our happiness.'

'I learned how wrong I had been when listening to that evil trio bickering amongst themselves. Bethany tried to blackmail you through greed... Gavin was angry about that, even though he instigated the rumour about you having sired Constance's child.'

William tightened his embrace to absorb her shuddering with his body.

'It was horrible listening to their depraved schemes. Time and again I prayed you would come for us. But I despaired of you finding us in time,' June whispered against his cheek. 'How on earth did you know where to look?'

'Isabel recalled that Blackmore had confided in you about his sister languishing in prison. Thank God you did disclose that to her, for it was from one of the turnkeys at the Fleet that I learned Bethany had told him about White Lodge.

'I had also sent an investigator to Devon to discover what he could about Constance's daughter. He uncovered unbelievably sordid details about Constance and the Blackmores. Bethany and Constance were unlikely partners brought together by a mutual dependency on vice. When details of their vile business, and especially Constance's proclivities, were uncovered the locals hounded them away. Poor Charlie Bingham must be turning in his grave.'

'What of the child?'

'She lives with her father's family now.'

June rose on an elbow to look enquiringly at him.

'The local clergyman has a pronounced limp. The girl has the same affliction. Apparently it has been an open secret since the child's birth that the vicar had cuckolded the lord of the manor.' He gave a short laugh. 'Apparently the villagers hold their minister in high esteem, it is Constance they despise for leading him astray. The reverend's wife was Christian enough to allow the child shelter in their home when her mother absconded to London with her colleagues.'

'They must have realised that the scandal would eventually catch up with them.'

'Oh, yes.' William choked an ironic laugh. 'They

knew that gossip and debt would catch up with them. Bethany was the first to fall foul of the duns. I imagine Constance was hopeful of luring a wealthy gentleman's protection to ease her path to a new life overseas.'

'And she chose you as her victim,' June said simply.

'That was her prime mistake,' William said. 'I might have had a reputation as a mild-mannered fellow, but I hope I am not a dullard.'

'I doubt people will think you placid now,' June said with some asperity. 'I could not wish for a more heroic husband.'

'And I could not wish for a more courageous and wonderful wife,' William said huskily. 'Sylvie is telling everyone that she owes you her life. It is marvellous that she has been so little distressed by it all. I think Adam is more affected. I have had to dissuade him from seeking out Carlisle. I have no liking for the old goat, but he cannot be hounded simply because he was nominated to ravish Sylvie.'

'We must not praise ourselves too much or perhaps we will again be deemed smug,' June said softly.

'I don't care if our contentment irks,' William countered vibrantly. 'We have each other and that is all that matters. Never again will I let us be pilloried. I have no intention of changing for anyone.'

'*I* feel different,' June said in a tone that harboured a secret, and her hands slid down to cup her abdomen.

William felt the sensation of her small hands moving between them. For a long moment his eyes devoured her face. 'Are you sure?' he finally forced out.

'No,' June replied softly. 'As yet I have no proof…no absence to convince me, but I *feel* so different.' She took his hands and touched them to her breasts, to her belly, as though he, too, must sense the wonder.

His hands travelled on and he smiled against her mouth. 'Well, until you *are* certain, there is still need to practise…'

Epilogue

'Lord Malvern, please come in. How nice to see you.'

If Edgar was unused to receiving such prominent members of the aristocracy at eight of the clock in the evening when well past the fashionable visiting hour, he admirably concealed his surprise.

Moments later when a track had appeared in the pile of his carpet and he learned the nature of the man's impromptu visit, his disbelief left him goggle-eyed for several long seconds. Finally he brought together his jaw well enough to burble, 'I'll fetch her mother.'

Gloria and Edgar Meredith exchanged glances. They looked at their eminent guest, who exuded a stubborn air of polished sophistication.

Edgar swallowed, then blurted out, 'You must

not feel obliged, sir, to do this just because you and she were alone in the dark for a short while. Exceptional circumstances were in play, and besides, nobody knows but us…the family. Good of you, though…very good of you, sir…'

'I should like to speak to her,' Adam said.

'She has not yet had her début,' Gloria whispered.

'By all accounts she does not want it,' Adam countered. 'It is not strictly necessary.'

'No, it is not,' Gloria agreed. Slowly it was dawning on her that what was occurring was not a mockery, but a miracle.

Adam read her expression and a half-smile tilted his lips. 'May I speak to her?'

Gloria looked at Edgar and, gaining little assistance from that quarter, made the decision to nod eagerly.

'Come away from the door, Gloria.'

'It's too quiet! Should I go in? It is highly irregular you know. I *should* go in…she is young…I am her mother…'

'She is seventeen next week. And for days past much in our lives has been irregular. Anyhow, who will know anything of it but us?'

Suddenly the door of the parlour burst open and Adam strode out. Without slowing his pace he managed to bow to Mr and Mrs Meredith and exit the house within less than a minute.

Edgar and Gloria stared at the parlour door, but their youngest daughter seemed determined to remain within. Tentatively they entered the room.

Sylvie was standing by the fire with her arms crossed over her waist and her soft lips under attack from her small teeth. On seeing her parents she stormed, 'He asked me to marry him. Why? All I expected was a ride in his curricle. I told him so and he said it was time I acted like a young lady instead of an infuriating brat. I don't even like him now.'

Edgar shook his head and blew out his cheeks. 'I'm going to my study,' he muttered.

Within a few moments of Edgar settling into his creaky chair and picking up his pen, Sylvie burst into the room, tears glossing her violet eyes. 'You must call him out, Papa. He said I was an infuriating brat. You must go after him now and tell him I hate him.'

Edgar took hold of a small, fidgety hand that was making disorder of his desktop. He gave it a calming pat before continuing to write in his ledger.

Sylvie stamped a small foot. 'You must! You must go after him and tell him I hate him. I want him to know.'

Edgar dropped his quill and looked up. 'In a year or two he will be back, my dear, then you can tell him yourself.'

* * * * *

0205/04

MILLS & BOON®

Live the emotion

Historical
romance™

THE BRIDEGROOM'S BARGAIN
by Sylvia Andrew

Minutes after her wedding to Lord Deverell, Alexandra is
brandishing a pistol at him, accusing him of ruining her father
and killing her brother! So Deverell makes her a vow to prove
his innocence. If after six months she isn't totally convinced,
then he'll take the consequences. What he must do now is win
Alexandra's trust – using *every* means at his disposal…

MARRIAGE UNDER SIEGE by Anne O'Brien

1643

With staunchly opposed political views, the new Lord and Lady
Mansell are not seeking love in a time of civil war. But Honoria
must appear loyal to Francis's Parliamentarian cause when their
castle is held under siege by Royalist forces. Yet amid the
devastation, passion is blazing between Honoria and her husband.
If only Francis could trust that his lady's loyalty were true…

MY LADY'S HONOUR by Julia Justiss

Upon meeting the lady who has bedazzled his best friend, Gilen
de Mowbry is surprised to find her hauntingly familiar. But
surely this demure ton miss can't be the mysterious Gypsy who,
for one unforgettable evening, danced for him in the firelight –
and who still taunts his dreams…?

REGENCY

On sale 4th March 2005

MILLS & BOON

All in a Day

What a difference a day makes…

CAROLE MORTIMER

REBECCA WINTERS

JESSICA HART

On sale 4th February 2005

Available at most branches of WHSmith, Tesco, ASDA, Martins, Borders, Eason, Sainsbury's and all good paperback bookshops.

0205/024/MB124

FREE

2 BOOKS AND A SURPRISE GIFT!

We would like to take this opportunity to thank you for reading this Mills & Boon® book by offering you the chance to take TWO more specially selected titles from the Historical Romance™ series absolutely FREE! We're also making this offer to introduce you to the benefits of the Reader Service™—

- ★ **FREE home delivery**
- ★ **FREE gifts and competitions**
- ★ **FREE monthly Newsletter**
- ★ **Books available before they're in the shops**
- ★ **Exclusive Reader Service offers**

Accepting these FREE books and gift places you under no obligation to buy; you may cancel at any time, even after receiving your free shipment. Simply complete your details below and return the entire page to the address below. You don't even need a stamp!

YES! Please send me 2 free Historical Romance books and a surprise gift. I understand that unless you hear from me, I will receive 4 superb new titles every month for just £3.59 each, postage and packing free. I am under no obligation to purchase any books and may cancel my subscription at any time. The free books and gift will be mine to keep in any case.

H5ZEE

Ms/Mrs/Miss/Mr...Initials ....
BLOCK CAPITALS PLEASE

Surname ....

Address ....

....

....Postcode ....

Send this whole page to:
The Reader Service, FREEPOST CN81, Croydon, CR9 3WZ

WIN a romantic weekend in PARiS

To celebrate Valentine's Day we are offering you the chance to WIN one of 3 romantic weekend breaks to Paris.

Imagine you're in Paris; strolling down the Champs Elysées, pottering through the Latin Quarter or taking an evening cruise down the Seine. Whatever your mood, Paris has something to offer everyone.

For your chance to make this dream a reality simply enter this prize draw by filling in the entry form below:

Name _____

Address _____

_____ Tel no: _____

Closing date for entries is 30th June 2005

Please send your entry to:

Valentine's Day Prize Draw
PO Box 676, Richmond, Surrey, TW9 1WU